When Ahdaf Soueif's first book appeared in 1983, it was acclaimed by the reviewers. 'To say it is promising is to understate the case', wrote Victoria Glendinning in *The Sunday Times*, and *The Observer* hailed an 'original new talent'. There was praise too from John Fowles and Edward Said, and *Aisha* went on to be named as runner-up for the Guardian Fiction Prize of 1983. It was a remarkable debut and when Ahdaf Soueif followed up with her magnificent novel, *In the Eye of the Sun*, her reputation in Great Britain, Egypt and the U.S.A. was triumphantly secured. Writing of *Aisha* in the *Times Literary Supplement*, Galen Strawson spoke of Soueif's gift for 'combining the style that her English experience elicits with the peculiarly Arab or Egyptian literary style in which she is already so accomplished a practitioner'. We now take that gift for granted. *Aisha* reminds us how it all began.

AISHA

Ahdaf Soueif

BLOOMSBURY

First published in 1983 by Jonathan Cape

This paperback edition first published 1995

Copyright © 1983 by Ahdaf Soueif

The moral right of the author has been asserted

Bloomsbury Publishing Plc, 38 Soho Square, London W1V 5DF

A CIP catalogue record for this book
is available from the British Library

ISBN 0 7475 2536 6

10 9 8 7

Typeset by Hewer Text Composition Services, Edinburgh
Printed in Great Britain by Clays Limited, St Ives plc

For
Fatma Moussa-Mahmoud

Contents

Returning

The little red car came speeding along the road and turned abruptly to park under a tree in front of a three-storey house. Nobody got out. The engine did not die. Then the car moved again; it backed out of the parking place, made a sharp U-turn and headed back the way it had come.

'I need those books,' Aisha told herself. 'I'm teaching a course and I need those books.' She drove to the main street then took a right turn. She drove straight on until she came to the roundabout. She circled the roundabout and came to a vast square. She knew she had come the right way but she did not recognise this square. She remembered a green garden with spreading trees and flower beds and paths of red sand. She saw instead a construction site. In the foreground was a large, squat, yellow mosque. On it was a placard and on that in large green letters were written the words 'The Mosque of Ismail'. She wondered who Ismail was and what degree of importance or wealth had obtained for him the planning permission to set up his mosque right here, in the middle of an area obviously designed as a recreation ground for the houses around it.

The red car went slowly up the east side of the square. Behind the mosque another building was coming up. The floors that had been completed were already greying as the rest were piled on top of them. A placard proclaimed the project: 'The First Islamic Institute in the Governorate of Giza'.

Between them, the Mosque of Ismail and the Islamic Institute took up five-sixths of the garden. Aisha looked at the strip that was left. The few trees were dusty and the grass was sparse and yellow. The whole place was strewn with bricks, cement, steel rods of varying lengths, and mounds of sand. There was no one about. It felt more like a demolition than a construction site. She wondered about the frogs they used to hear at night. And the crickets. Where had they gone? Had they all moved into the one-sixth of semi-garden that was left? And what did they do about territorial rights? How could they co-exist in such a drastically reduced space? But then, maybe they didn't. Maybe the strong had overcome the weak and a race of superfrogs was now living in the remains of the garden. The builders of the Mosque of Ismail and the First Islamic Institute in the Governorate of Giza were helping evolution along.

The road was bumpy and dotted with potholes. Some of the potholes were full of stagnant water. Aisha looked around her. She remembered a bright winter day, a motor-scooter wobbling under her as she tried to ride it down a smooth road. Finally, it had collapsed on to its side and she had fallen, one leg caught under the little Vespa. Everyone had run to her but she had picked herself up and tried again. She looked around. You'd be mad to try to learn to ride a motor-scooter down this road now.

She arrived at the top of the square. Six years ago their house had been the only one along the north side. Pretty, in five storeys of reddish-brown and beige, it had looked over the garden. Now it was flanked by tall apartment blocks and so stood diminished, looking bleakly out over the dusty road and the Pepsi-Cola kiosk that had sprung up on the pavement in front of it.

Aisha looked around for a place to park. There were no trees to cast any shade and one side of the road was much like the other. She pulled the car over to what used to be the kerb and stepped out into a sand heap. She shook the sand from her shoes. The curious heads hanging out of windows were still there, but now a number of them were covered in the white Islamic head-dress that was spreading so rapidly. Did they belong to the same people as six years ago? Or different? Younger sisters, perhaps, daughters? Out of the corner of her eye she could not tell. Ignoring them, as she had always done, she walked purposefully in.

The tall glass doors were still there. Miraculously, they had not yet been broken. The marble-floored lobby was clean but there were no plants in the pots and there were cigarette ends on the dry, cracked earth. A strange man in a striped *galabiya* was sweeping the marble floor. She wished him good day. He answered sullenly, leaning on his broom, waiting for her to pass.

'Are you the doorman here now?' she asked.

'God willing,' he replied briefly.

'Where are Abdu and Amna?' she persevered.

'Abdu? They took him into the army long ago.

And Amna has gone to live with her folk in the village.'

'Oh.'

She started climbing the stairs. She wanted to ask more. Had Abdu and Amna finally had their much-desired baby? Or were they still barren? What had Abdu done about learning to read? They had been incorporated into her dream of coming home, these two. She had even gone down to Mothercare and looked for Babygros for Amna's longed-for child.

Repeatedly she had imagined in detail the scene of her homecoming. It would be the beginning of the academic year, a warm October day. She would drive up to this door with Saif. Abdu would jump up and come running out, wearing his broad grin and his white peasant's underwear, his eyes and teeth shining in his dark face, crying, 'Praise God for your safe return, Set Aisha!' He would grab her hand and try to kiss it while she protested and insisted on shaking his hand. 'How are you, Abdu? How are you doing? And how is Amna?' And, hearing the noise, Amna would look out from the room below the stairs and, seeing her, come out tying her coloured kerchief round her hair, her slow, shy smile spreading over her pretty face. And she too would praise God for her safe return and ask, 'Have you come to stay with us for good now?' And when Aisha answered 'Yes,' Amna would say, 'You fill the house with light.' They would carry her cases upstairs. They would all have to make two journeys because there would be a lot of luggage after such a long stay abroad. Later, she would unpack and come down to give Abdu and Amna their presents:

for Amna a dress length of coveted, brightly patterned synthetic material with the trimmings and buttons to match, and for Abdu a watch. And if there were a child . . .

She had arrived at her floor. The passage was dark. The old worn-out key was ready in her hand but she could not see the keyhole. She stretched out her arm blindly and the key immediately fitted into the lock. Is it coincidence? she wondered. Did I just happen to find the lock? Or does my hand remember? She turned the key. It was a little stiff but the door opened. She felt a surge of irritation. Typical. Going away for two weeks and not bothering to double-lock the door. Then she remembered. It's nothing to do with me.

She pushed the door open and a forgotten but familiar smell met her. She stood still. It couldn't be. She had always thought it was the smell of fresh paint and that as the flat grew older it would vanish. For the year that they had lived in the flat it had constantly been there and she had thought, 'With time it will go.' Time had come and time had gone and the smell was still there. Maybe he'd had the flat repainted? Her hand, moving along the wall, found the light switch. No, it had not been repainted. The walls were the same: olive green on one side, beige on the other. It must be a ghost smell, she thought. Like a ghost limb. When they cut off your legs you go on feeling the cramps in your toes. Only now, they are incurable. I'm smelling fresh paint because I'm used to smelling it. It's not *really* here but I'm smelling it.

Her eyes travelled along the entrance hall and fell on the white marble basin in the middle of the green living-room wall. A sheet of cardboard had been laid across it and balanced on it were some telephone directories. What plans they had had for it. It was to be a small fountain, the wall behind it to be inlaid with antique ceramic tiles and its pedestal surrounded by plants in large brass urns. They had had to wait; a question of money. But the basin had been there. It was the very first thing they had bought for the house. Wandering down the old bazaar one day, they had found it thrown carelessly into the dusty corner of a junk shop. The owner had wanted ten pounds but they had got it for eight. All three pieces: the basin, the back panel, and its pedestal. They had carried the heavy marble carefully to the car and later she had made enquiries about getting it scoured and polished. Someone recommended a shop in the old part of Cairo and she had gone with her mother-in-law. When they got there it turned out that the man specialised in cleaning tombstones. Saif's mother had been shocked and urged her not to leave the basin with him. But she had laughed. No omen could dim her happiness, no headstone mar their future and she had left the marble basin to be cleaned among the winged angels and the inscribed plaques. Later, it had been fixed – with its beautiful shell-like back panel – into the green wall. And sometimes she had filled it with water and put in it a small machine which made a miniature fountain. It had always delighted their friends and she had sat on the black rocking-chair and watched it for hours.

She craned her neck. The rocking-chair was there. In exactly the same position she had left it six years ago: angled by the french windows under the smaller book-shelves. A present from her white-haired professor of poetry, it had arrived three days after the wedding with a huge bouquet and had immediately become her favourite seat.

She stepped inside the flat and closed the door quietly behind her. It needed oiling. The handle was hard to turn. She faced the darkened flat and felt it tilt. She headed quickly left down the long corridor to the bathroom. She did not switch on the light but crouched in front of the toilet, retching. She wondered whether the cistern worked. It did. That had always been a good thing about the flat: they'd never had trouble with the plumbing.

Washing out her mouth she glanced up and saw her reflection dimly in the large mirror hanging beside her. She looked. It had been part of a Victorian hallstand which she had found in a junk shop and he had declared hideous. So they had compromised: the top and bottom of the stand had been cut away and disposed of and the mirror with the intricately carved frame now hung suspended on the wall. She switched on the light, then went back to the mirror. The reflection staring back at her was not the one she was used to seeing there. The changes moved into focus. A slimmer face framed by shorter, more curly, though still black, hair. A string of now-taken-for-granted pearls shone round her neck. She fingered the pearls. She remembered a hotel bedroom in Paris and the wonder and delight when the pearls were thrown into her lap as she sat up in bed. He had created Paris for her. As he had created Rome. Then he had stopped. Brussels, Vienna, Athens. They were all untouched by his magic. Why? They had still been together. She shook her head. Her expression too was different. The wide-opened, open, expectant look was gone. Instead there was – what? Repose? Something that people took for serenity. But she knew. She knew it was frail as an egg-shell. She shook her head again and looked around. The shower curtains and matching bits and pieces had been bought in Beirut. Such a tight budget. And onion soup: her first taste of *Soupe à l'onion gratinée* eaten with Melba toast in the Hotel Martinez at one o'clock in the morning as they'd planned their shopping list for the next day. She had loved it. The thin strands of the *gratinée* stretching as she pulled the spoon away from the dish, the Melba toast crisply cutting through them. Could it all come back again? she wondered. She stroked her pearls.

She put her hand out to the mirror. She lightly traced the outline of her face with her finger. But the mirror was a wall between herself and the warm flesh behind it. She could not feel the contours of her face: the nose marked no rise, the lips no difference in texture. And it was cold. Her finger still on the mirror, it came to her that that was an apt metaphor for her relationship with him. She could see him, sense his contours and his warmth but whenever she made a move to touch him there would be a smooth, consistent surface. It was transparent, but it was unbreakable. At times she had felt he put it there on purpose and she had been furiously resentful. At others it had seemed that he was trapped behind it and was looking to her to set him free. She stood very still. Twice in the year she had lived in this flat she had locked herself in here: squeezing herself into the corner behind the door and crying till she could not breathe. Twice he had not come looking for her and when she had finally crept out, exhausted, she had found him comfortable within his cloud of blue smoke in the living-room, reading, with Bob Dylan on the record-player. The bad times seemed to have been a succession of bathrooms. Hotel bathrooms all over the world had seen her locked in, head over the loo, crying, or simply sitting on the tiled floor reading through the night while he slept alone, unknowing, in large double beds that mocked her.

She turned and walked back through the corridor to the living-room. The cane-backed sofa and armchairs sat quietly in the dark. She crossed over to the sofa and sat down, feeling again the softness of the down-filled, green-velvet-covered cushions. She examined them closely. The feathers were still escaping from the seams. Years ago, she had thought, 'In a couple of years all the feathers will have gone!' But here she was, six years later, and they were still there and still escaping. She looked around. The books were all in place. Economics and electronics to the left, art and literature to the right, and in the middle, history. The paperbacks were in the smaller bookcase that had been built into the wall. On its lowest shelf were the records. There were far more albums there now than before. And the music centre was new too. The old, battered record-player had ended up with her. Together with a few of the old records.

She lifted her eyes to the wall above the music centre. Her portrait had gone. Painted when she was twenty-one and given to them both as a wedding present, he had vowed he would always keep it and when he had a study

11

of his own he would hang it there. Now it hung in her parents' home; in her father's study. In its place was an old Syrian tapestry. It showed the Arab knight and poet Antar on horseback and his beloved cousin Abla in a litter on a camel's back. Abla had been on a journey and Antar was proudly escorting her back to their settlement. His horse pranced with tail swishing and neck arched high and Abla peeped coyly out to smile at him from behind the canopies of her litter. On one side were inscribed the verses:

> And I remembered you
> When battle raged
> And as lance and scimitar
> Raced for my blood
> I longed to kiss
> Their glinting edges
> Shining like your smiling mouth

and on the other:

> I am the lord's knight
> Famed throughout the land
> For a sure hand with the lance
> And the Indian sword.

They had bought it in Damascus. One day, wandering down the labyrinth of narrow streets that made up the covered market surrounding the Ommayad Mosque they had come across a tiny shop selling fabrics and tapestries. They had gone in and spent time looking over the materials and she had spotted this one in black and gold. She had laughed as she showed it to him. 'This could be your motto. He thought a lot of himself, like you.' For a moment he had been defensive. Then he had trusted in her good faith and laughed and bought it.

Her remark had been true. He lived in heroic proportions and would have been better off as some medieval knight, be it Arab or Frinji. He would have gone out and slain dragons and ghouls and rescued damsels in distress. He would have been kind to his squire and his horses and would have believed in the chastity of his wife weaving in her tower. And perhaps, in the Middle Ages, his belief would not have been misplaced.

Another memory sprang to her mind. 'The Spartans,' he was fond of saying, 'spent the last day before Marathon adorning themselves and combing their hair. They knew they were going to die.' On their last day, he had come up to the living-room in the cottage. His car had been packed. He was setting off down the M1. He was drunk. But he was very well dressed, with a velvet jacket and a silk foulard. 'I have combed my hair,' he had said quietly, swaying at the top of the stairs.

She pressed a hand to her head. Not again. Please. Not again. It's over now. Finished. Her eye caught her desk. It was cluttered with objects. She stood up and went over, looking at them absently. Papers, letters, ashtrays, an old half coconut shell, a silver flask in a leather case, some flying instruments salvaged from a wrecked plane, and a gun. She picked it up. An old Colt .45, serial number **91. 'When you shoot yourself in the head,' he had told her, 'your brains splatter all over the place. It's a hell of a mess.' 'What can you do?' she had asked. 'Put your head in a plastic bag first.'

The doorbell rang. She stood very still. It rang again. She walked slowly to the door and opened it. A boy stood holding a carefully folded pile of shirts. He handed them to her. She took them automatically.

'How much?'

'Twelve shirts by five piastres is sixty piastres,' he said.

She went back to the living-room, put the shirts on the sofa and took her purse from her handbag. She took out seventy piastres and went back to the door.

'Take these.'

'Do you have anything else for ironing?'

'No thanks,' she replied, 'not today.'

She closed the door and turned again to face the flat. The dining-room was now directly opposite her. She walked over. These had been her favourite pieces of furniture. Solid dark oak in a 'rustic' style with carved lions' heads for handles. The massive table and sideboards stood waiting for her in the gloom. She opened the small, upright sideboard they had used as a bar. It was as well stocked as ever and the crystal goblets sparkled quietly inside. She put out her hand. She had treasured these goblets and the formal china with gold and green edging. She looked around. The table would be covered with the beige and gold damask tablecloth and the room lit by candles in silver candlesticks. Where is the silver? she wondered. The trays and candlesticks were not in their places on the sideboards. She started looking for them. She opened the sideboard doors and peered inside, and there were the delicate little blue and white Japanese bowls. Bought in Tokyo. A great tiredness overwhelmed her. She put out a hand behind her, dragged up a chair and sat down. The whole world. What city was left that she could go to and not find memories? Why not give in? Why not come back? Tokyo. All those pretty little girls in red miniskirts and white cotton gloves operating the elevators and incessantly bowing – 'Thank you for shopping at our store, we hope you have a good day, we hope you will come back.' All those gaudy shrines, presided over by sleepy-eyed Buddhas who had sat inscrutable as she clapped her hands and tied a piece of paper with a wish to the sacred tree. She had always wished for one thing. Incoherently. Make it right. Dear God, Buddha, Allah, make it right. She felt the pricking of tears behind her eyes but she would not cry. Two whole years had passed since that day in the living-room of the cottage and she was not going to cry any more.

She resumed her search for the missing silver and in a corner of the larger sideboard she found it. She drew it out. Trays, ashtrays, candlesticks and a trophy inscribed 'Miss Cairo University 1970'. Eight years ago . . . All were tarnished. Bits of them were quite black. Typical again, she thought. He can't bear to see them tarnished and can't be bothered to get them polished so he tucks them away in a corner and hopes they'll disappear. Or maybe he even hopes that by some miracle when next he thinks to look he'll find them gleaming and bright. She rubbed a corner of the cup with her thumb. I wonder if he has any polish? she thought again. With a surge of energy she made for the kitchen. She stood looking around. His mother had bought them the kitchen fittings and her aunt had made the curtains. So pretty, with their blue flowers and white broderie anglaise trimming. They were still there, the sunlight shining gently through them. And there was the breakfast bar and the little two-eyed cooker where she'd learnt to make goulash soup. She looked at the sink. There were two unwashed glasses. She took off her rings and watch and started to wash them. They'd always had friends around. Parties. How had she managed with such a tiny kitchen? Such a tiny fridge? She opened the fridge. Even the containers had been carefully chosen and had blue flowers to match the curtains. In the door were two bottles of beer and a bottle of white wine and seven eggs. She opened a round container. It was full of jam. She dipped a finger in it and licked. Date jam. His mother's date jam. She had a vivid image of him: a serious little boy of seven, playing in the sea at Alexandria. His nanny wades out from the beach holding up her *galabiya* with one hand, the other holding out a sandwich. She waves and calls, 'Come out now, come and have a date jam sandwich!' When he was seven she had not yet been born, but the image was vivid in her mind from stories repeated by his mother every time she gave her a present of a large jar of date jam. She made it with her own two hands. The dates were laid neatly one on top of the other and in the centre of each one was an almond and a clove. Then they were covered with syrup. 'It always brought him out,' she would say. 'He loved the sea, but he loved his mother's date jam more.' And she would laugh.

She put the lid back on the pot and closed the fridge

door. Where were those photos of him as a child that she had had framed? They were not hanging anywhere. But then he had never been particularly keen on them. She remembered the silver. She rummaged around in the kitchen cupboards. She found some shoe polish and some powdered soap, but that was all. She closed the cupboard doors and went back to the dining-room. Slowly she put the silver back into the corner of the sideboard. I could buy some, she thought. I could go right now and buy some polish and come back and do it. She closed the sideboard door and looked up at the wall above it. There they were. The framed maps of Sinai. The two old army maps he had used when he made his celebrated trek across the desert. He had gone with a friend. They had travelled by jeep and by camel, spending days at the monastery of Saint Catherine and weeks with the Sinai Bedu. She had listened wide-eyed to his tales of that trip. 'Can we do something like that together?' she had asked. 'But I've already done it,' he had said, laughing. And it was true. He had already done it. He had already done a lot of things. His memories were more vivid to her than her own. She had no memories. She had had no time to acquire a past and in her worse moments, locked up in some bathroom, it had seemed to her that his past was devouring the present.

She pulled herself away from the deserts and mountains and turned to the living-room. Her eyes fell on the pile of fresh shirts on the couch. She crossed over and picked them up carefully and walked automatically to the wardrobe in the corridor. She pulled open the lefthand door and sure enough, there were the shelves of clean ironed shirts. She put away the ones she was carrying. The whites with the whites and the coloureds with the coloureds, noting as she did so how many were unfamiliar to her. Then, on an impulse, she pulled open the righthand door. Suits and jackets hung quietly in place. At the end of the row was a fur-lined overcoat they'd bought at Harrods. 'Your fur,' she used to call it. 'Who's sitting warm inside his fur?' And he'd always grin and pull the collar up around his neck. She put out her hand and stroked it, then started to pull it out. Behind it, something hung shrouded in a white sheet. She left the coat and, taking hold of the other hanger, removed the shroud. She found herself looking at her wedding dress. It hung from her hand, a dream creation in white and grey lace, embroidered lovingly with tiny seed pearls. Her hand shaking, she hung it back in the cupboard and hung the sheet over it. She knelt down to adjust the sheet round the train and her fingers hit a smooth object. She pulled it out. A white cardboard box. She knew instantly what it was. Hesitantly she opened the lid, and sprang up and back with a scream. Her veil and small, pearl-embroidered Juliet's cap nestled in tissue paper. They were covered with black moths. Trembling and with cold hands, she put the lid back on the box and carried it to the kitchen. She put it in the sink, searched for the matches and set fire to it. She stood and watched it burn, then she cleared up the ashes and washed the sink and her hands. Her stomach turned again and again she rushed to the bathroom. Always bathrooms. She flushed the toilet and rinsed out her mouth, then she slowly made her way to the bedroom. She pulled herself up on to the large four-poster bed and lay there, careful to keep her sandalled feet off the fine pink linen sheets. She lay still as the world pitched and tilted and, weakened now, she felt the tears creep sideways from her eyes on to the bed. This too was familiar. Lying there, dizzy, weeping, sick. Recurring illnesses which, they said, were hysterical. 'What's wrong with you?' they asked. 'Why don't you settle?' She didn't know, she always said. She didn't know. She lay on the bed and sobbed herself to sleep, carefully keeping her feet over the edge.

The instant she woke she saw the velvet-papered walls and the white lace curtains. She did not have an instant's doubt about where she was. She knew. What she did not know was *when* she was. What happened? she asked, lying on the bed. Where is he? What did I dream? She lifted herself up on one elbow and saw her reflection in the dressing-table mirror. She did not see a round-faced girl with long, straight black hair. Instead she saw the woman with the curly hair and the pearl necklace. She looked at the mirror with recognition, relief and sorrow. She lowered herself gently off the bed, straightened it, and left the room.

She went to the living-room and headed for the righthand side of the large bookcase. She scanned the literature shelves and picked out five books on seventeenth-century poetry. Then, carrying the books, she picked up her handbag. She walked through the flat and out of the door. She switched off the light and pulled the door to. Then she put her key in the lock and turned it firmly, twice.

Aisha

Out in the sun, she got into her little red car. She put the five books and her handbag on the passenger seat and drove down the west side of the square. She manoeuvred carefully round the potholes till she came out of the bumpy road and to the roundabout once again. There she picked up speed.

1964

I stood in the snow, freezing and waiting for the bus. I was lonely. I had woken up at six as usual, washed and dressed in the cold dark while my young sister and brother slept on. I had poured myself some cornflakes, smothered them in sugar and eaten them. Then I had let myself out of the back door and walked to the corner of Clapham High Street to wait for the thirty-seven.

The snow was deep around my ankle-high, fur-lined, black suede boots inherited from my mother. Or rather, I suppose now, donated by my mother while she wore ordinary shoes in the snow. Fourteen, with thick black hair which unfailingly delighted old English ladies on buses ('What lovely, curly hair. Is it natural?') and which I hated. It was the weather; hours of brushing and wrapping and pinning could do nothing against five minutes of English damp.

I loved Maggie Tulliver, Anna Karenina, Emma Bovary and understood them as I understood none of the people around me. In my own mind I was a heroine and in the middle of the night would act out scenes of high drama to the concern of my younger sister who had, however, learnt to play Charmian admirably for an eight-year-old.

We had come to England by boat. My father had come first. My mother had had trouble getting her exit visa. It was the New Socialist era in Egypt and there had been a clampdown on foreign travel. Strings were pulled but a benign bureaucracy moves slowly and it was two months before we were allowed to board the *Stratheden* and make for England.

We got on at Port Said. The *Stratheden* had come through the Suez Canal from Bombay and before that from Sydney. It was full of disappointed returning would-be Australian settlers and hopeful Indian would-be immigrants and beneath my mother's surface friendliness there was a palpable air of superiority. *We* were Egyptian academics come to England on a sabbatical to do *Post*-Doctoral Research. I wasn't post-doctoral, but it still wasn't quite the thing to play with the Indian teenagers, particularly as among them there was a tall, thin, seventeen-year-old with a beaked nose called Christopher who kept asking me to meet him on deck after dark. In a spirit of adventure I gave him my London address, and paid for it when he actually wrote.

I was summoned into my parents' room, where the letter lay on the desk. It was addressed to me and had been opened. It never occurred to me to question that. It said that it had been respectfully fun knowing me and could he meet me again? It had a passport-size photograph of him in it. My parents were grave. They were disapproving. They were saddened. How had he got my address? I hung my head. Why was it wrong to give him my address? Why shouldn't I know him?

24

How had he got my address? I scuffed my shoes and said I didn't know. My lie hung in the air. Why had he sent me a photograph? I really didn't know the answer to that one and said so. They believed me. 'You know you're not to be in touch with him?' 'Yes.' There were no rows, just silent, sad disapproval. You've let us down. I never answered his letter and he never wrote again – or if he did I never knew of it.

I was not troubled by the loss of Christopher. Just by the loss of a potential adventure. Anything that happened to me in those days represented a 'potential adventure'. Every visit to the launderette was brim-full with the possibility of someone 'interesting' noticing me. When I slipped and sprained an ankle, the projected visits to the physiotherapist seemed an avenue into adventure. But the old man massaging my foot and leering toothlessly up at me ('What a pity you don't slip more often') was more an ogre than a prince and after one visit my ankle was left to heal on its own.

The likelihood of my actually arriving at an adventure was lessened by the eight-thirty p.m. curfew imposed by my parents ('Even in England it's not nice to be out later than that, dear'). But no path to rebellion was open to me so I waited for something to happen obligingly within the set boundaries.

Days of calm Clapham harmony passed and I was fretting – 'moping', my mother would say. Nothing ever happened. Life was passing me by. Then one day, when I returned from the launderette, my mother said that some young people, the Vicar's children from down the road, had come by and asked if I would like to go out with them that evening. She had said yes for me. I was thrilled.

They came to collect me. Two tall and angular girls with vanishing eyebrows and hair pulled back into pony-tails and a boy with extremely short hair and glasses and a brown check suit. My knowing heart made a little motion towards sinking, but I was resolute. I was going out with three 'young people of my own age'. I did not know where we were going but the possibilities were infinite. We might go down to the café at the end of the road and play the juke box; I had looked into the window and seen it gleaming. We might go to a movie ('It's called a "film", dear'). We might go to a youth club; I had heard of those and imagined them to be like the Gezira Club at home, only much more exciting and liberated. Instead, we went to church.

It was not even an old and picturesque church. It was modern and bare and the benches were miles away from the pulpit and my new friends' father preached for a long, long time. I told myself it was nice that they thought nothing of taking me, a Muslim, to their church. It was proof that I belonged – a little; that I wasn't as different as I feared I was. We all prayed. I knew about prayers from books I had read and made the appropriate movements, and when we bent our heads and closed our eyes, communing silently with God, I prayed for something to happen to relieve the awful tedium of life. I knew it was slightly incongruous to ask for excitement in church, but I was desperate.

'Friends.' The Vicar suddenly spoke. 'In our city today we find increasing numbers of people who come to us from far places: from alien races, alien beliefs. There are some of those among us tonight. Should any person in this congregation wish to join with us in the love of Jesus Christ, let them raise their hands now while the eyes of everyone are closed in prayer and I will seek them out later and guide them into the love of Our Lord. Raise your hand now.' I kept my eyes closed tight and my fists clenched by my sides. I could not swallow. There was no doubt in my mind that he meant me.

Afterwards we all had tea in a hall somewhere in the building. Everybody was large and pale with straight light brown hair and tweeds. I felt excessively small and dark and was agonisingly conscious of my alien appearance, and particularly my alien hair, as I waited to be sought out and guided into the love of Jesus Christ. Mercifully, it did not happen. Even so, I had been – however unknowingly – betrayed, and I knew I would never go out with the Vicar's children again.

On the way home I kept my eyes open for the Teddy boys and the Rockers preening themselves on the street corners. My heart yearned after them, with their motorcycles and their loud and gaily-coloured girlfriends. They were all that I was missing and every time I walked past one, my heart would thud in anticipation of his speaking to me. It was hopeless, I knew. My parents would never allow me to make friends with them. And when a crowd of them whistled at me one day, I knew it was even more hopeless than that. For they were hostile. And I realised that with my prim manner and prissy voice they wouldn't want me for a friend anyway. I was a misfit: I had the manners of a fledgling Westernised bourgeois intellectual and the soul (though no one suspected it yet but me) of a Rocker.

After I had refused a few times to go out with the church children ('But you're always moping around complaining you don't know anybody'), temporary rescue came from some friends of my parents. We went to visit them and it turned out that they had a son three years my senior. They suggested (I was sure to his annoyance) that he take me to the theatre. My parents had no choice but to give their consent there and then, and arrangements were made for later in the week. Oddly though, I still had to get formal permission to be out late. Permission to go to the theatre apparently did not automatically include that. After all, one could always get up in the middle of the first act and be home by eight-thirty. However, permission was granted, but at ten-thirty on the dot I had to be home. I bathed myself like a concubine in our sit-down bath and went out dressed to kill in white gloves and a tartan kilt. There were lots of awkward silences. *Hobson's Choice* ended at ten. David suggested we have something to eat but I had to get from Waterloo to Clapham in half an hour, so food was out. There followed a rush to get home and though he kissed me goodnight in our front garden he never asked me out again. But I had had an adventure: my first-ever kiss. I had felt nothing at all, but I became more and more a heroine and borrowed from the library Mills and Boon romances which I read by torchlight under the bedcovers in the dead of night.

By now my parents had decided that the best thing to do with me was send me to school. I was meant to be studying at home for my Egyptian Prep. certificate at the end of the year, but at school I would use all my time constructively. I would also meet people my own age and make friends. I looked forward to it. I had always been happy at my school in Cairo and had no misgivings about this one. Besides, schools in books like *The Girls' Annual* all seemed jolly good fun. Because of their liberal, enlightened ideology and that of their friends and advisers, my parents decided to put me in a comprehensive – in Putney.

So, here I was. It was early '64. The Beatles yelled 'I wanna hold your hand' and shook their long, shiny black hair and their hips; the Mods and Rockers zoomed through the streets in their fancy gear; and I stood in the snow on the thirty-seven bus stop, on the outside, looking in.

My first contact with school was with the dark cloakroom lined with rained-on navy blue coats, berets and boots.

My second was with the long, windy corridor you had to walk through without your coat to get to the main body of the school.

My third was with thousands of uniformed girls in a huge hall singing about fishermen.

No one had warned me it was a girls' school. I had always been in a mixed school at home and found boys much easier to get on with than girls. Suddenly school didn't seem like such a good idea; a vast, cold place with thousands of large girls in navy blue skirts.

'You can be excused from Assembly on grounds of being Mohammedan,' whispered the teacher who had brought me there. No fear. I wanted nothing more than to merge, to blend in silently and belong to the crowd and I wasn't about to declare myself a Mohammedan, or even a Muslim, and sit in the passage looking bored and out of it with the Pakistani girls wearing their white trousers underneath their skirts. 'It's all right,' I said. 'I don't mind.'

My attempts at fading into the masses were unsuccessful. During the first break I was taken to Susan, the Third Form leader.

'Where you from?' She was slight and pale with freckles and red hair.

'From Egypt.'

'That's where they have those Pharaohs and crocodiles and things,' she explained to the others. 'D'you go to school on a camel?' This was accompanied by a snicker, but I answered seriously,

'No.'

'How d'you go to school, then?'

'Actually, my school is very near where I live. So I simply walk.' As I said this I was conscious of ambiguity (I even knew the word for it): I had not made it clear that even if school were far away I still wouldn't go on a camel. I started again:

'Actually, we only see camels – '

'D'you live in a tent?'

'No, we live in a Belgian apartment block.'

'A what?'

'An apartment block owned by a Belgian corporation.'

'Why d'you talk like that?'

'Like what?'

'Like a teacher, you know.'

I did know. I knew they were speaking Cockney and I was speaking 'proper English'. But surely I was the one who was right. My instincts, however, warned me not to tell them that.

'How many wives does your father have?'

I bridled. 'One.'

'Oh, he don't have ten, then? What does he do anyway?'

'Both my parents teach in the University.' A mistake this, one I would live to regret; I was affiliated to the enemy profession.

'Oh, teachers are they?'

'In the *University*,' I supplied.

'Sarah's Dad's an engineer. He makes a hundred pounds a week. How much does yours make?'

Sarah's Dad was obviously the financial top dog in the Third Form. But what was I supposed to say? Nothing, actually, he lives on a grant? But don't you see, we're intellectuals, we're classless? You can't ask me such a vulgar question?

'I don't know.'

'Well, d'you have bags of money?'

I heard my mother's voice:

'We spend our money on travel, books, records, on *culture* . . .'

This was met with silence. Then:

'D'you have a boyfriend?'

Again I heard my mother's voice:

'I know boys who are friends.'

'D'you have a special boyfriend?'

I thought quickly. David hardly qualified as my boyfriend. But, for status, I lied:

'Yes.'

'D'you kiss him?'

'Do I what?' I stalled. I didn't really want to share that. And something told me it would unleash other questions I wouldn't be able to answer.

'D'you kiss him?'

'No.'

'D'you sit on his knee?'

'No.'

'Well, how far have you got then?'

'We went to the theatre,' I said. They lost interest at that point. Just moved on and never paid me much attention again. There was a girl there with blue eyes and straight black hair and her second name was Shakespear. I could have made friends with her, I thought. But she was Susan's best friend and I would not compete.

School was a disaster. The white girls lived in a world of glamour and boyfriends to which I had no entrée. The black girls lived in a ghetto world of whispers and regarded me with suspicious dislike. I was too middle of the road for them. There was one girl of Greek parentage, Andrea. She came home with me one day. She came into our kitchen as my mother was preparing dinner. 'Cor blimey!' she cried. 'Olives. Can I have one?' Smiling kindly, my mother pressed her to take several. But to me she seemed unmitigatedly gross and although I was polite to her, I could not make myself be her friend.

Academically, it wasn't much better. I only scraped through most subjects and was terrible at maths. I couldn't understand why at the time because I was doing fine with the maths I was studying at home on my own. Looking back, I realise it was because I didn't know the terminology in English. The teacher was a harassed, birdlike man in white shirtsleeves, with huge eyes swimming behind his rimless spectacles, and he looked so helpless that it never occurred to me to ask him for help.

As for brilliance, I could not have chosen an unluckier subject to excel in: English. The class would have forgiven me outstanding performance in science or sports, but English? And Mrs Braithwaite, with her grey bun, her glasses over sharp, blue eyes, her tweed suit hanging lower at the front than it did at the back, booming out, 'The Egyptian gets it every time. It takes someone from Africa, a foreigner, to teach you about your native language. You should be ashamed.' At first I was proud and thought how dumb they were not to know that birds of a feather 'flocked together', that worms 'turned' and that Shylock wanted his 'pound of flesh'. But as the hostility grew I realised I had made another mistake. I tried to fade into silence, but it was no use. Those sharp, blue eyes would seek me out and she would call me by name, and I was not humble enough to give a wrong answer or say I didn't know.

Meanwhile, at break, I wandered round the cold playground, yearning for my sunny school in Cairo, and soon I learnt to smuggle myself into First Lunch where I would quickly bolt down shepherd's pie and prunes and custard, then slink off to the library. There, hidden in a corner, holding on to a hot radiator uninterrupted by cold blasts of air or reality, I communed with Catherine Earnshaw or pursued prophetic visions of myself emerging, aged thirty, a seductress complete with slinky black dress and long cigarette holder with a score of tall, square-jawed men at my feet.

At sports time, however, I was not so lucky. I clambered nimbly enough up and down ladders in the gym but we often had to go out on to the playing fields for games of hockey. Why hockey? I asked. Why not tennis, or handball? No. Hockey was the school game and that was what we played. The weather was cold and grey and damp. The cold made my bones chatter, the grey depressed me and the damp made my hair curl. The hockey sticks terrorised me. I had visions of them striking my ankles, my legs, bare and goosefleshed in my gymslip. I lurked on the sidelines, shivering and protecting my legs with my hockey stick. There was no escape. And it was too cold to dream.

My parents were satisfied. I could not admit failure or disappoint them by telling them I was miserable at school so I dwelt on the treasures in the library and my achievements in the English lessons with a smattering of information on films we watched in history and geography. The rest, when questioned, came under the broad heading 'O.K.'.

As a mark of approval, I was given a tiny Phonotrix tape recorder with which I taped songs from *Top of the Pops* and *Juke Box Jury*. I taped them through the microphone and the sound I got was terrible, but I could hear through the distortion and I played 'Can't Buy Me Love' and 'As Tears Go By' incessantly.

Music was magic to me and every day as I walked home from the bus stop I would peer through the net curtains at the juke box gleaming against the wall in the corner café. It was a dark, different world in there; there were square tables with plastic covers chequered in green and white. On each table were plastic pots of salt, pepper, mustard and tomato ketchup. At the tables sat silent old men in cloth caps and jackets and shirts with no ties. One day I pushed open the door. There was a single chime and I walked in.

My heart was pounding and I couldn't see very clearly at first. The counter at the far end floated in a haze. I walked up. A large man in a striped apron stood behind it. I put a shilling on the counter and asked for a cup of tea. He pushed sixpence and a cup of tea back at me. I carried them over to a table in the corner and sat down. When I had got my breath back I stood up again and walked over to the juke box and studied the titles. Here I was on familiar ground. I put in my other shilling and selected three records. I didn't drink my tea. It was strong and white and not like the tea I was used to at home. But I was happy. When the songs were over I walked out and went home. I never told anyone about my adventure. But every three days, when I had saved one and six from my pocket money, I stopped on the way home at the corner café, bought tea I never drank, and played the juke box. The Beatles, the Stones, the Animals, Peter and Gordon, Cilla Black, the Swinging Blue Jeans, the Dave Clark Five. I played them all. And for the duration of three songs I was happy and brilliantly alive.

My secret bursts of life at the corner café sustained me

but at school things got steadily worse. The atmosphere in English was becoming intolerable and I could hardly believe my own stupidity at maths and science. My hiding place in the library was discovered and I was often yanked out and deposited in the middle of the playground. My legs got knocked with the hockey sticks anyway. The white girls lived their lives and the coloured girls lived theirs and I hovered on the outskirts of both. Then, one day, the St Valentine Dance was announced.

I was terror-struck and elated. All these girls would turn up in their designer clothes with their sophisticated boyfriends. They would glide with ease on to the dance floor and do the Shake. Would I be a wallflower? Unwanted? Again the odd one out? I never dreamed of not going. The world of glamour, passion, excitement and adventure was going to be revealed for an evening. It was going to come within my reach and I would certainly be there to grasp it.

I obtained permission to go to the dance, and Very Special Permission to stay out until eleven o'clock. I asked David, the only boy I knew in London, to come with me. My mother bought me my first pair of high-heeled shoes: '*le talon bébé*' the style was called, and the heels were just one and a half inches high.

February 14th finally arrived. My hair was shining, my turquoise silk dress with the high Chinese collar was enchanting and I had nylon stockings and high-heeled shoes. David came to fetch me in a dark suit and had a Pepsi with my mother before we left. He had borrowed his father's car, so we drove to Putney in style. I played it cool, as though, for me, every night was St Valentine's night, but in my head was a starry, starry firmament.

We got to school and made our way to the Assembly Hall. School was transformed. It was no longer dull and cold and hostile. It was vibrant, throbbing, every door, every corridor leading to the magical place where the dance was to be held.

It was eight o'clock as we walked into the hall. The lights had been dimmed and the loudspeaker was beating out 'Come right back, I just can't bear it, I got some love and I long to share it,' and nobody was on the dance floor. All the girls were there. They were in party clothes and stood grouped together at one end of the hall. At the other end, huddled in tight, nonchalant groups in dark suits, were the boys from Wandsworth Comprehensive, our sister school.

The situation slowly sank in. None of the girls had brought a boy with her. After all the grave talk about kissing and sitting on knees, no one had actually brought a boy with her. They were all standing there, tapping their feet and hoping that the boys from Wandsworth would ask them to dance. And the boys were nervous, pretending they didn't know what they were there for, and chatting to their mates.

We joined some girls from my class for a while but conversation was awkward and we ended up standing alone by the wall. I tried to enjoy the music but it felt dead and flat. David asked me to dance but I knew he was being dutiful and besides I was too shy to be alone with him on the floor.

Time passed as I hung on waiting for something to

happen while the evening slowly crumbled away and the stars went out one by one. I knew now there was no hidden world, no secret society from which I was barred. There was just – nothing.

A week later I stood as usual at the bus stop in the cold morning. I waited a few moments for the thirty-seven, then I turned back and walked home. When my mother woke up she found me sitting in my school clothes in the kitchen with a fresh bowl of sugared cornflakes in front of me.

'Aisha! What's the matter? Are you ill?' she asked.

'No,' I said.

'Well, what's the matter? Why aren't you at school?'

'I'm not going to school any more.'

'What?'

'I'm not going to school any more.'

'Have you gone crazy? What's the matter with you?'

'I'm studying for my Egyptian Prep., aren't I? I'll concentrate on that.'

'But why won't you go to school?'

'I don't want to.'

'But why?'

'It's just not worth it.'

'But you liked it so much –'

'I hated it.'

'What on earth will your father say?'

'. . .'

'He'll be very angry.'

'I'm not going to school any more.'

She told my father. She carried back protests, even

threats: 'Daddy is terribly displeased with you,' then, 'Daddy won't speak to you for weeks.' Withdraw all your love, I thought. I won't go back. They went against their principles: 'You won't get any more pocket money.' It was still no good.

Every morning my parents went to the University and my sister and brother to school. I would draw up my father's large armchair in front of the television, carry up some toast and butter, and watch the races. Or I would switch on my Phonotrix and dream. Or read. The whole house was my territory from nine in the morning to five in the afternoon and I lived my private live and was impervious to the cold, disapproving atmosphere that pervaded the evenings. After a couple of weeks they gave up.

One day I discovered a secret cache of books hidden in my parents' bedroom. *Fanny Hill, The Perfumed Garden* of Sheikh Nefzawi and the *Kama Sutra*. My rebellion had paid off in grand style. I spent my fifteenth year in a lotus dream, sunk in an armchair, throbbing to the beat of the Stones, reading erotica.

And I passed my exam.

The Suitor

'*Mais, chérie, parle,*' begged Mimi's mother. '*Elle est ton amie, n'est-ce pas? Elle doit choisir, n'est-ce pas?* Really, *chérie, je ne sais plus que faire.* I don't know what to do with her. Her uncles are getting so nervous . . .'

Tante Safi was wringing her hands. She wore a bright printed cotton house-dress that buttoned down the front, the last button being at mid-thigh. Her street clothes were consistently a sedate black so it was always a little shocking to come upon her in her flamboyant housecoats.

'Nobody is good enough for her. Nobody fills her eye. The cream of young men have come knocking at her door and she just won't give them a chance . . .'

She sat framed in the deep brown sofa, her slim white legs crossed at the knee, angled delicately sideways with the feet pointed. Although I had known Tante Safi for years I was still fascinated by her hands, arms and legs; they belonged to an attractive woman in her twenties. They were sensuous, delicately boned, even fragile, with a pale, translucent, unblemished skin. It was always with surprise that my eyes, travelling along them, past the black or brilliant clothes, came finally to rest on an aged and wrinkled face with downward-slanting, tired, grey eyes, a wart and a frazzle of peppery hair.

'If her father had been alive, it would have been different. But her uncles are responsible for her and they are starting to ask questions: What is the matter with her? What is it she's waiting for? *Qu'est-ce qu'elle attend?*'

I glanced up for the hundredth time at Marianne's father hanging on the wall in a heavy gilt frame edged with a black ribbon. He had a wide grin and his head was tilted rakishly sideways as though he were enjoying a good joke.

Tante Safi leaned forward earnestly. 'Don't hold it against me, *chérie*, but since that scandal with Sahar we have *les mains sur le coeur*. If anything like that should happen it would kill me, it surely would . . .'

Sahar, Marianne's cousin, had married a Muslim. Her father and uncles had cut her off completely and behaved as though she were dead. Or rather, as though she had never existed. Her name was never mentioned. Her mother and aunts continued to see her secretly; fraught, desperate visits for they were sick with fear for her. Under Muslim law her husband could divorce her at any moment and then, cast out from her family and her people, where would she go? What would she do? Her world would be inconceivable. Tante Safi now had constant nightmares about Marianne. There were far more Muslim than Coptic men in Egypt, and besides, the most eligible young Copts were emigrating en masse to Canada and the U.S.A. Marianne's mother did not want her to emigrate.

The doorbell rang and Tante Safi went to answer it.

Mira, Marianne's young neighbour, rushed in. 'Well, Mira, welcome,' said Tante Safi, trying to smile. 'How's the bridegroom?'

'They're fine, Tante,' replied the girl breathlessly. 'Tante Safi, I've come to ask a big favour. You know Marianne's tan shoes? Can I borrow them for tonight? They go so well with my velvet jacket. I'm going out with Nabeel tonight and as I get out of the car I know he'll be looking at my legs and those shoes make my feet so pretty . . .'

'Take them. I'm sure Mimi won't mind. You know where they are. Go in and take them.'

When she had gone, Tante Safi came back to the sofa. This time she sat on the edge. 'You see how it is, Aisha? Time passes, *chérie*. I am getting old. Soon I won't be here for her any more. What will she do then? Will she live on her own? And one has to think of children. Mimi isn't getting any younger. You *must* speak to her, *chérie, pour moi . . .*'

Marianne had turned twenty-nine. She had inherited her mother's delicate limbs but combined them with her eldest aunt's hips and thighs. Her top half was slim with round, full breasts and tapered into a small waist which flared out into broad hips and heavy thighs. One might have thought that her body was out of keeping with itself but the truth was that her particular combination exuded a powerful sexuality of which she, for a long time, was unaware. She had light brown hair and fine eyebrows arched over sleepy, deep-set eyes. Since her father's death fifteen years ago, she had shared a bed with her mother.

'What is wrong with *this* suitor? He's respectable and comes from a good family. A doctor and well-off with his own private practice, a flat in Zamalek and an Audi. And he's dying for her, ready to do anything. *Qu'est-ce qu'elle veut de plus?* Please speak to her. She'll be home soon. I have to go to church, then I'm spending the afternoon with her sister. My grand-daughter has a bad cough. Please, Aisha, wait for her and speak to her.'

The shutters had been closed against the sun and the windows against the noise of the street. The white gauze curtains hung unmoving to the floor. Everything in the darkened room was exactly as it had been when I first walked in here ten years ago: the oak furniture, '*style anglais*', with deep, soft cushions; the crystal ashtrays and flowerless vases; the good Persian rug on the tiled marble floor and the ancestral photographs, in the centre a large print of Tante Safi herself in full wedding-dress, her train and veil swirling around her feet and into the frame.

I waited until Tante Safi was a safe distance down the road, then I quietly let myself out. It was no use waiting for Marianne or trying to speak to her.

I knew what Tante Safi was doing right now: wringing her hands and complaining bitterly to the priest of Mimi's inexplicable behaviour. Father Boulos had many roles in the close-knit community and one of them was that of matchmaker. He sent round numbers of upright young men who made appointments to come and inspect Marianne. Most of them went back to him and made formal proposals which she then turned down. The priest might have got tired of the recalcitrant bride long ago, but he received a handsome premium from her family for every potential bridegroom he produced so he kept up the supply of suitors.

Marianne established rigid conditions, without which she would not even see the suitor. Certain professions were unacceptable; doctors always had affairs with their women patients; academics (unless they had a private income) did not make enough money; people in the hotel business mixed with the wrong set. Any man more than ten years her senior was too old.

When a suitor did get an appointment to come and see her, he had to promise to come alone, without a friend or a mother. And she promptly tore him to pieces.

Ears were one of her favourite targets. Her criticisms ranged from prosaic to the fanciful: they flapped, or they were too fleshy, or red, or they looked transparent, or brittle, or as if they'd been pinned back against his head when he was a baby; and sometimes they were just plain grubby.

Trousers were another: one man wore his trousers too low ('Who does he think he is, James Dean?'); another wore them too high ('He looks like Charlie Chaplin'); some wore them too baggy, others too tight; some too flared, others not flared enough; while one unfortunate wore turn-ups at a time when they were, strictly speaking, out of fashion.

Shoes, too, were a highly significant item. If they were not mirror-like she was displeased ('Doesn't he have a servant to clean them?'); if they were slightly scuffed or even if they had a heel-piece ('Doesn't he have the money to buy a new pair?'); moccasins were out ('They're lazy, like bedroom slippers'), and so were lace-ups ('Too old-fashioned, conservative'). The only shoes she would tolerate were slim, square-toed ones with discreet stitching and side buckles.

If a man's appearance and clothing were passed, he was given a chance to speak. Most of them, trying to impress a family they had been sent to by the priest, said the wrong things. They assured Marianne of their respect for and devotion to their families ('Tied to his mother's apron strings'), of their virtuous characters and blameless habits. One man admitted he 'occasionally' went to the cinema. Mimi had visions of herself incarcerated in a two-bedroom flat with a husband who fell asleep after supper. 'I want to live,' she would cry. 'And here a woman only starts living after she's married. I want someone who enjoys life, who knows *how* to live. Someone who'll take me to lots of parties and to all the hotels and restaurants. Someone who'll stay up all night. Otherwise I might just as well stay at home with my mother.'

On the rare occasions when Marianne could find no immediate fault with the suitor, her mother, unaccountably, would pounce: 'A successful psychiatrist? He's going to emigrate to America, mark my words. He'll want to take Mimi away from me and what would I do then? No, no, he won't do.' Another time: 'A graduate of a technical college? *Mon Dieu*. My daughter is a university graduate. How *can* she marry a man from a technical college?' Gently, friends would try to point out that a third-grade arts degree, obtained with difficulty, did not argue a budding Wittgenstein and that the man was putting his technical education to lucrative practical use. It was no good; Marianne had to marry someone with, at the very least, a Master's: '*Il faut avoir au moins une Magistaire*. Otherwise she might despise her husband and that would never do, would it, *chérie*?'

We discovered things about Cairo we had never known before. One man, an engineer with a Fiat and a good income, had a house in Heliopolis. 'Mimi cannot live in Helipolis,' declared her mother. 'It's too far away.'

'But he's put his car and his chauffeur at her disposal, Tante. And of course, at yours too, to go and visit them.'

'Heliopolis water is no good,' she finally said. 'It's bad for the stomach and Mimi has a delicate stomach. It won't do.'

Father Boulos did not mind. He went on producing new candidates and getting his fee. Mimi and her mother developed a terrifying reputation and many young men did not dare take the step of calling on them at home. Instead, they would go to the American library where Mimi worked. She grew adept at smelling out a suitor from a genuine reader. Her back would stiffen, her eyebrows arch and she'd rap out to her assistant, 'Gina, would you look after the gentleman, please?' 'But, Mademoiselle Marianne –' the gentleman would begin. But it was no use. He was left with Gina to take out a membership of the library while Mimi disappeared into an inner sanctuary till he went away.

The years had gone by. Those of her Muslim friends who had got married were now getting divorced and the current joke was that Mimi had taken the simpler route to the single state. But no one was really convinced. We all still waited for the, by now, thirty-ninish man with the M.A., car, flat in Zamalek or Garden City, business, money, well-cut trousers, polished, buckled shoes, and acceptable ears. Tante Safi had sick headaches and days in bed. Clan disapproval grew stronger with every day and with every younger cousin who got married or engaged.

But, although her family did not know it, ten months ago Marianne had acquired a reason for her behaviour, her waiting. A man had walked into the library. He was fortyish and wore a well-cut beige suit which later turned out to be a genuine St Laurent. He had thick black hair with a touch of grey at the temples, shrewd brown eyes and a wide mouth with thick lips and large teeth. He took out a membership as Engineer Wassef Ghali, establishing himself a Copt, and disappeared among the bookshelves. Marianne was intrigued. He wore no wedding ring and he was in the library at eleven in the morning, so he did not work in the government. He must either work for a foreign company or run his own business. His clothes looked expensive. He must be doing well. He did not behave like a suitor, or was he just clever? When he left she looked out of her window and saw him climb into a red Volvo.

A week went by before he appeared again. He nodded briefly to the girls at the desk and made for the reference section. Once he came back with a question, but he addressed it to Gina.

By the time he had been to the library three times, Marianne's interest was fully aroused. So when he happened to be leaving once at closing time and offered her a lift home to Zamalek she did something she would normally never have done: she accepted. She climbed into his car and on the short drive home he asked questions about herself, her family, her work, addressing her directly as 'Marianne' without the usual polite 'Mademoiselle'. Sitting near him, his hand on the gear lever close to her, she was, for the first time in her life, aware of being attracted to a man and she was conscious of her body and her legs as she climbed out when he opened the car door for her a few blocks away from her home.

Ten days later he invited her out to lunch and took her to the Rôtisserie at the Hilton. She started inventing excuses for not going home at lunchtime and for being late in the evenings and a web was woven in which the friends covering up for her were caught. Meanwhile Tante Safi wrung her hands and Father Boulos went on producing suitors.

At first Marianne thought Engineer Wassef Ghali might be a suitor playing a clever game. Then she grew convinced he wasn't. But she was happy. She had never liked the traditional method of introduction. She had always wanted to know that her bridegroom was in love with her; that he had not merely been looking for a suitable bride. She had always wanted to be attracted to a man, to fall in love first, then marry later. And Engineer Wassef Ghali seemed to be everything she had dreamt of. So she waited, sure he would propose in his own time. And meanwhile she went out with him and took risks undreamt of in her community.

He had a flat in Zamalek and she took to meeting

him there. Her reputation would have been ruined had anyone found out. But then it would have been ruined had she been seen with him in a public place. So she bribed the doorman and argued that she was, in fact, taking the lesser risk.

At first she was afraid of him and afraid that he would lose respect for her; would think her 'easy'. But he treated her in the flat as he treated her outside it and she grew bolder and more confident with each visit.

It was so different from her home. Everything here was modern: all chrome and glass and white leather with shag pile rugs and dimmed lights and mirrors. Marianne moved into this new world and took possession. She cooked for him and they ate together in an easy informality. He never seemed to be too busy for her, never had any pressing engagements, and when she questioned him he simply said he had good people working for him. He wore Eau Sauvage and sat around the flat in trousers and a short silk *robe de chambre* and let her follow her own moods and do as she pleased until she grew completely relaxed, then a little unhappy and neglected, wondering why he never touched her.

Engineer Wassef Ghali sat on the sofa and watched Mimi at the other end of the room, leafing through his records. Aznavour was singing '*Les enfants de la guerre ne sont plus es enfants*' when he very quietly said, 'Marianne?' She half turned to look at him. 'Leave those and come over here.' He had commanded and she obeyed. He took her hand and drew her down till she was on the floor between his knees, facing him. He leaned forward and traced her cheeks softly with his fingers, looking intently into her wide-open eyes. He cupped her head, his fingertips pressing at the back of her neck. 'Listen. Are you listening to me?'

'Yes.'

'I promise I shan't harm you. You must trust me. Relax with me and I promise I shall do nothing to harm you.' As she gazed up at him he bent forward and kissed her gently on the forehead, then on the temples, then on her closed eyes and her cheek and just below her ear, then inside her ear and back to her cheek, then, chastely, on her lips. As her lips parted his fingers wrapped hard into her hair, pulling her head back, and his tongue pushed into her mouth.

She was in love. She could no longer sleep in her mother's bed and moved out and into the spare room. Tante Safi was more distressed than ever, the corners of her grey eyes drooping lower and her French becoming more and more insistent.

Marianne was now spending all the time she could at the flat. She knew this was no way to behave. She knew that if her uncles found out there would be undreamt-of trouble. She knew she should play harder to get if she wanted her lover to propose to her. But she could not help herself. He was a man of the world and knew how to treat her. She knew that the reason behind his manner, his confidence, must be the amount of experience he had had, and though it pained her to think of him with other women, when he said, 'Sit in that armchair and take off your blouse, slowly, and your bra . . .' she obeyed. Her body was beyond her control and subject only to his will. He was her dreams and fantasies come true and he seemed to be familiar with them, making her play them out in the opulent, nouveau-riche luxury of his flat.

He introduced her to pleasure and to pain; and to pleasure through pain, handling her body freely and making it his own. He possessed her so completely that it became physically painful for her to be separated from him and she grew thin and pale and had black rings under her eyes.

Yet he never actually penetrated her. All her training, her conventions, her instincts made her draw away if he ever appeared to be approaching that point. However she felt, whatever she did, she had to remain a virgin for her wedding night. And he never pressed her. She wondered often whether that was because she pleasured him enough or whether it was because he had other women whom he met at night. His answer was always that the love she gave him was enough. 'And besides,' he would add, 'didn't I promise never to harm you?'

Months went by and the longed-for proposal never came. Marianne was feeling the strain of her situation; she wanted to be his wife, to be always with him; she hated leaving him in the afternoon; spending the evenings with her mother, fending off suitors and wondering all the time where he was and what he was doing; sitting with nerves stretched through family conferences on the subject of her marriage.

She hinted to him of the risks in their unconventional arrangement. He assured her no one would find out. She told him of the pain it caused her to leave him every afternoon. He made love to her and comforted her. She asked outright if he had been married before. He said he had not. She thought maybe he had disreputable or socially inferior parents. She questioned him about his family. He was evasive. She decided that must be it: he did not propose because he was ashamed; he knew that her uncles would make enquiries concerning him, that they would find out about his family background and refuse him. And he did not want to lose her.

Six months had gone by when she decided to take her sister into her confidence. Her brother-in-law was a kindly man, high up in the police force, and perhaps he would agree to play the mediator. Her uncles respected him. He could persuade them not to find fault with Wassef's family and convince Wassef himself to come forward and propose. He need not know how well she knew him. She could just say he came to the library often.

Medhat, her brother-in-law, listened to his wife then went off to make his enquiries. He had a friend in the secret service and he approached him for information. The friend went to work and dug up a file. It appeared that five years ago Engineer Wassef Ghali had been accused of attempting to bribe a high government official in order to obtain a contract. The charge never stuck but it directed attention towards him. He was now suspected of having some connection with a vice ring. He was seen in the company of prostitutes and it was known that he ran three flats: one in Zamalek, two in Garden City. The flats were under surveillance and tabs were kept on all the people seen going in and out. The friend produced a list of people seen around the flats and Marianne's name was on it. Medhat was horrified. He managed to persuade his friend to erase her name from the list but he had been badly humiliated and he went home to his wife exploding with rage.

'What kind of family is this I've married into? Have you no menfolk? Have you no respect? You see how it is? You see the company she keeps? She actually goes to a man's flat. A whoremaster. God only knows what she does there. This is the result of all this "freedom" and "going out to work". She's going to ruin all our reputations. Absolutely. *All* our reputations . . .'

Suzanne could hardly believe it. Mimi? A relationship with a man? Involved in a vice ring? Prostitutes? It was unthinkable. But she sensed that her own marriage was in danger and worked hard to pacify her husband. The first thing to do was to end the relationship. With great difficulty she dissuaded Medhat from rushing straight to their uncles with his story. She argued that the main thing was to avoid scandal. A great family upheaval would be terrible and if the uncles came into it there was no knowing where it would all end. Marianne's name was no longer on record. He had seen to that. Why didn't he speak to the girl on her own? She would surely be frightened enough to listen to him and do as she was told.

Medhat spoke to Marianne. She was utterly shocked and completely disbelieving. She kept begging him to meet Wassef and ascertain for himself that a mistake had been made. He said that if he met the man he would shoot him; he would meet him with a pistol, with a pair of handcuffs . . . Finally, in the face of his threats to tell her uncles and of what they would do to Wassef ('We'll hound him out of the country. We'll have him in gaol on a dozen charges'), she promised never to see him or have anything to do with him again.

It was a promise she had no intention of keeping. Despite the careful watch Medhat and Suzanne kept over her, she managed within a few days to arrange an appointment. She would not go to Wassef's flat but met him at the Meridian coffee bar instead. After some chat and a cappuccino she gently led up to the subject by asking how many flats he had. His face changed as he asked what she meant. 'I just wondered,' she answered. 'Someone said they saw you going into a flat in Garden City at midnight.'

'I was visiting a friend,' he replied.

He dropped her. Completely. Days and then weeks passed. He never phoned. He never appeared at the library. When she tried phoning him there was never any reply and when, desperate, she went round to the flat the doorman said the Engineer had 'gone away for a while'. Now she had been waiting four months. Hoping her absence would move him. Hoping he would miss her; would learn that he could not do without her.

Meanwhile, the atmosphere at home strained with tension. Her uncles were no longer speaking through her mother but directly to her; she was the only woman still unmarried in the family and she was a liability; she was almost thirty; she should choose now, while she still had the chance. Her mother and aunts repeated again and again that pregnancy and giving birth were much more difficult and dangerous after the age of thirty. Medhat added his pressure. Privately, he reminded her of the lists he had seen. He had taken her name off one but there might be others. When the police moved in on that dog – as they definitely would – if questions were asked, her name might come up and then where would she be if she had no husband to protect her reputation? What would her uncles do to her? Who would ever want to marry her after that?

A few days after she had asked me to speak to Mimi, Tante Safi phoned.

'*Chérie? Je te bien remercie. Elle a accepté –*'

'What?'

'*Elle a accepté.* She has accepted a suitor.'

'Who is he?' I asked.

'He is a professor of economics,' said Tante. 'But he has a private income, of course. He used to be in the University of Alexandria and has only recently moved to Cairo, so he doesn't have a flat. That is, not in Cairo. He has a lovely flat in Alexandria that they can use for the summer vacation. They have such long vacations at the University, *tu sais*. In Cairo, he will move in with us. He is forty and comes from a good family in Menia and has a Peugeot 504. He doesn't want Mimi to work any more –'

'But why?'

'He wants her to have children. And Medhat agrees with him. Medhat approves of him completely. It's so good when brothers-in-law take to each other, *n'est-ce pas?*'

'Congratulations, Tante,' I said.

Naturally, I went to the engagement party. The flat sparkled, the vases were full of flowers, the ancestors hung serenely on the walls. Mimi's father smiled above the heads of the friends and relatives who thronged busily around. Marianne herself was beautifully made up and coiffed and wrapped in a long golden sheath. The bridegroom seemed pleasant enough. He treated her with admiration and respect, like a dozen men she had refused before. He gave her a diamond ring, a bracelet and a *collier*.

'But are you not the littlest bit happy?' I pressed, cornering her in her room where she was rearranging her hair.

She shrugged into the mirror. 'He's all right.'

'He seems kind,' I offered.

She shrugged again. 'He's all right.'

'Are you really going to live *here*? With your mother?'

'Yes. Of course Mamma will move into the spare room. This room will be redecorated for us.'

'Don't you want somewhere new? Somewhere private? Somewhere of your own?'

'No. Besides, this is convenient. Mamma can help me look after the children.'

'Well, he really seems to care for you,' I said uncertainly. 'How d'you feel about his ears?' trying to revive our old joke.

She shrugged a third time. 'I didn't notice.'

'Marianne,' I suddenly begged, 'Marianne, why have you accepted him?'

She turned to look at me. 'Why not? I can't wait for ever. And besides, what is there to wait for?'

Knowing

I remember a time of happy, dappled sunlight. French windows open on to a flowering garden. From the garden gate to the open windows runs a paved and sloping pathway and at the top of the pathway stands a bright blue tricycle poised for the dizzying, exhilarating glide down the path. All you had to do was get it to the beginning of the incline and lift your feet off the ground and whoo – away you went. You had to pull up smartly or you ended up inside the living-room.

The living-room has huge, faded armchairs and coloured rugs and lots and lots of books. The walls are covered with them. Some have pictures, some you are allowed to pick up and look at, some are not to be touched. All are to be treated with great respect and never torn or folded or scribbled in or put face downwards or looked at while eating in case you drop food on them. In the middle of the books sit the grown-ups.

The grown-ups are wonderful. They drink tea and smoke and laugh and talk all the time. The women are beautiful with red lips and fingernails. The men are tall and handsome. They all do clever things. They write books and make music and paint pictures. Their pictures blaze on the walls of our apartment.

Looking back, I see a pool of sunlight, and in it, a child. She is dressed in a blue and white spotted frock with a white lace bodice. She holds on to her mother's skirt. Seized by a sudden fit of shyness outside the door of the living-room, she sucks slowly at her thumb. But then, coaxed and encouraged, she ventures in and is immediately picked up and cuddled and kissed to a chorus of 'Darling'. 'I've got to paint her. I've simply got to paint her,' cries Uncle Sameer, as he does every time and, reassured, she tosses her hair back and smiles up at him. Yes. The grown-ups are wonderful.

And clever. And wise. They can do anything, explain everything. The child is lying in her bed. Every time her mother puts the light out a horrible creature with long curving arms appears on the ceiling of her room and she screams. Her mother comes back in and switches on the light, but she can see nothing. After a bit she calls the father. He, too, can see nothing but he lies down beside her. Her mother switches off the light and closes the door. He sees the creature on the ceiling. 'It's the shadow of the chandelier, little goose.' He comforts her and shows her how it moves when the chandelier moves and explains about light and shadow. She is safe.

Yes. The world is safe and pleasant and the worst grief I know is to be beaten at snakes and ladders by Uncle Murad. He moves my counter slowly down every curve of the final, fatal snake and I watch, lips trembling, on the verge of tears, till my father intervenes and carries me off.

Knowing

My father is a psychologist. He is very strong. He can crack nuts by pressing them in his hands. When we play in the garden he can run very fast. He runs very fast in circles. He runs so fast that I can't catch him. But after a bit he slows down and I am able to run up to his legs and hold him tight.

The garden is always sunny. I play with my blue tricycle or eat my meals sitting in a wide-eyed rocking-duck. This is my home. I know the address by heart.

Near my home there is the club. My nanny, Dada Zeina, takes me there most afternoons. In summer I swim. At other times I play on the swings. Sometimes I have a magazine or a picture-book. I sit on the grass beside Dada Zeina and look at the pictures. She chats to the other nannies but I am absorbed in the pictures.

In an older part of town there is another house that I go to often. There, too, I know the address by heart. It is older than our house and the rooms are bigger and higher. In the centre of a high-ceilinged room full of sunlight, a woman is kneeling on a red and blue prayer mat. Her hands are folded one over the other. Her eyes are closed. When they are open they are a deep green. Underneath her flowing white head-dress, her hair is a long, soft, light brown. Beside the prayer mat, the slippers she has taken off stand side by side. They are flat and made of crinkly pink leather with a tiny rosette on each toe. I sit close by on the floor solemnly watching the familiar ritual. This woman is my grandmother. My mother's mother. 'Mama Hajja', I call her: Mama who has gone on the pilgrimage to Makkah. It is a title of respect. But it is also a truthful description. For Mama Hajja has been to Holy Makkah. Although she was delicate and her health was frail, she had gone. She had travelled alone, my grandfather (her husband) having had neither the time nor the inclination to accompany her and look after her. Her lips move as she nears the end of the Koranic verses she is reciting and she slowly bends over to prostrate herself, her forehead touching the floor between two open palms. The broad, loved back is too great a temptation and I steal up from the floor and clamber on to it. Mama Hajja makes no sign that anything untoward has happened. When it is time, she slowly straightens up. I try to hang on but I tumble off her back and on to the floor behind her. I wait. I know that soon it will be time for the second prostration. Sure enough, within a minute she bends over, forehead touching the floor, and in a flash I am again on her back. She recites 'God is Great' three times slowly, then slowly straightens, tumbling me once more off her back. I settle on the floor behind her. She recites the final Greeting to God and Mohammad and his family and children and all the prophets that God has ever sent. She turns her head to salute the angels at her right and left shoulders and, almost in the same movement, reaches for her slipper. She stretches an arm behind her back and makes a grab for me but I am small and quick and crouch just out of her reach, laughing. She turns and starts for me, in her hurry and irritation forgetting to stand up but coming after me on hands and knees, brandishing a pink slipper. I dart away, reeling with laughter and pointing my finger back at her and suddenly she sits back on her heels on the sun-flooded, polished wooden floor and starts to laugh too. I wait a few seconds to make sure it's safe, then rush back to fling myself into her open arms. 'You little monkey. You would have made me break my prayers?' I snuggle contentedly against her breast in the sunlight, sucking my thumb. In my parents' house naughtiness is frowned upon. So is sucking your thumb. I name this other one 'the Spoiling-House'.

Now it is a sunny winter's day and I am playing in my grandfather's shop. It is a prospering furniture shop with his name, 'Morsi', emblazoned in gold Diwani script across the front. It stands on Morgan Street, the street forming the western border of the central market-place in old Cairo. The market is a fascinating place with its high glass ceiling, its stacks of vegetables and pyramids of oranges, guavas and Lebanese apples. It is slightly frightening too, with thousands of slaughtered chickens hanging open-beaked above the live ones who continue to scurry around, clucking mindlessly. The gutters between the stalls run with mud and blood, but people sit on little wooden stools drinking sweet tea and swishing the flies away with graceful horse-hair fly swats.

I am not allowed to go into the market-place on my own but I have the run of my grandfather's shop. The furniture on the ground floor is arranged for display. Gilt armchairs standing in a circle make a drawing-room in the shop window and I sometimes sit here for hours gazing at the world outside: the meat vans unloading in front of the market-place, the carts trundling in with fresh vegetables from the villages. I stare out at the shoppers as they stare in at the gilt drawing-room.

Aisha

Upstairs there is a loft used for storing furniture. You go up a set of creaky wooden stairs without banisters. It is dark. There is one feeble lamp but its circle of light serves only to make the place more ghostly. There is a well in the middle of the floor, and from it you can look down into the shop. This loft is Paradise. The furniture is all tumbled together and in the gloom I create caves under huge desks and labyrinthine castles in piled-up sofas. The only thing I am forbidden to do is get inside the cupboards. Occasionally, I tiptoe into one and sit, knees to my chin, huddled in a corner, feeling both frightened and brave. But I never dare close the doors and engulf myself in total darkness.

Above this loft, arrived at by a different stairway, is the workshop: huge, marble-floored rooms filled with the smell of varnish and the blare of the radio. A broad, sunny terrace overlooking the market-place; stacks of wooden armchairs and desks waiting to be polished; and all my grandfather's workmen: carpenters, upholsterers and varnishers who carry me on their shoulders and buy me sweets and Sport-Cola.

I have been playing in the loft when I hear them call my name.

'Aisha! It's lunchtime! Come down!'

I run down the stairs just as the boy from the neighbouring restaurant comes into the shop carrying a large, round brass tray shining in the sunlight. On it is a sheep's head festooned with parsley and surrounded by little dishes containing the various salads and dips. In one corner of the tray there are five round loaves of bread. In another there are three bottles of Cola. There is only one empty plate. The boy puts the tray down on a table between my grandfather and his friend, Sheikh Zayed.

'Got everything you want, Am Morsi?'

My grandfather checks that the bread is hot and the drinks are cold and nods, waving his hand to dismiss the boy. He is a man of few words.

I sit on a swivel desk-chair with two cushions under me and Sheikh Zayed tucks a napkin round my neck. They put the empty plate in front of me. 'In the name of God, the Compassionate and the Merciful.' The two men start breaking up the sheep's head with their fingers. They shred off some lean meat and put it on the plate in front of me. My grandfather hands me a fork. I want to eat like them with my fingers but I know it's not allowed. *I* must eat with a fork. They eat in silence, occasionally putting a titbit on my plate or in my mouth. And we drink our Cola and dip our bread in the salads.

My grandfather is a big man with greying hair and sharp, black eyes. He has large workman's hands and a gruff voice. Myth surrounds him: how his father died when he was six and his uncles usurped his land; how he trekked from his village in Upper Egypt to Cairo at the age of seven and found work in the central market; how he built up his business and became fabulously wealthy; how he rejected the trappings of wealth and rode in overcrowded buses where a thousand pounds at a stroke were picked from his pocket. He does not pray and is not known to be religious. Nobody ever calls him 'Hajj' or 'Sheikh'. They use 'Am' for respect instead. They say he is a hard man but I, his first grandchild, do not find him so. I know that if I choose the right moment and dance for him, singing,

> I come from Upper Egypt
> Like my father before me,
> And my Grandad too,
> He comes from Upper Egypt

his face will break into a wide smile and he'll give me a brand new pound note.

Now, we finish eating and the boy comes to take the tray away. He brings with him two nargilas: one for my grandfather and one for Sheikh Zayed. I love watching the coals glow red and the water bubble as my grandfather pulls on the mouthpiece. I wait: I know that in time he will offer it to me. After a few puffs he does and I pull and pull but I can't make the water bubble. He laughs and brings out his snuffbox. It is beautiful, engraved silver glinting in the sunlight. He takes a pinch and offers me the box. I am delighted. I know what he expects and I am happy to play the clown. I take a pinch of snuff and put it to my nostril. After a second I break into three exaggerated sneezes and my grandfather and Sheikh Zayed burst out laughing. I jump down from my chair and my grandfather catches me and wipes my face with his large white handkerchief with the blue border.

By the Place of Abdin, there is another house that I remember. And another set of grandparents. I don't go there as often as I go to Grandfather Morsi's, but when I do go it is to stay a few days. There are no uncles here, only two aunts, and it is much quieter and darker than in the other house. Here, I call my grandmother 'Neina' and I would not dream of climbing on to her back while she prayed. However, sometimes, at night, she will take the net off her hair and it will fall down her back long and soft, black threaded with silver. Then she will let me kneel on the sofa behind her, and brush it carefully and gently.

Yes. To everything there is an order and a pattern. And the pattern and the order are good. Time, from one birthday to the next, runs gently by, overflowing with an abundance of pleasures. If there are fears or griefs, they are minor and I am always able to be comforted by the grown-ups.

It is my birthday, I am five years old. In the morning I go with my grandfather to Groppi's to order a three-tier chocolate cake with coloured sugar rabbits and five blue candles. I also get a bar of Swiss chocolate. In the afternoon I go down on an errand with my Aunt Soraya and spot a cart loaded with wooden bathroom clogs. I want a pair. 'No,' says my aunt. 'Daddy won't like it.'

'But I can keep them in the Spoiling-House,' I say, already practising subterfuge. Eventually she gives in and buys me a pair. 'I want to wear them now.'

'You can't wear them in the street. They're only for the bathroom.'

'I've seen people wear them in the street.' I look around. A little beggar girl is coming towards us

71

wearing a pair. 'There!' I cry. 'There! She's wearing clogs!'

'But she's a little beggar girl,' protests my aunt. It is no
use: I am down on the pavement, unbuckling my shoes.
I clatter proudly back to my grandfather's in socks and
clogs. When evening comes I am surrounded by uncles
and aunts and presents. My grandmother has made me
a pink tulle bridal dress with a long veil and train. I wear
it happily. But I also keep on my clogs.

Then there are all the festivals. On the Prophet's
Birthday the streets are filled with bright stalls selling
sweets. Sugar knights on horseback for boys, sugar dolls
for girls. The doll stands, arms akimbo, in a flared dress
and a high bonnet of coloured and silver paper. She has
painted black eyes and eyebrows and red cheeks and lips
and stands in glory on the sideboard till the ants get her
and she crumbles into decay beside her knight.

And Ramadan lasts a whole month. A month of winter
evenings spent round the fire cracking nuts and roasting
chestnuts. A month of exotic sweets and communal
breakfasting at sunset. Of waking up at four in the
morning (even though I do not fast) to join in the
last meal before daybreak. Later to be tucked up again
with a fresh hot-water bottle. A month of playing with
a coloured lantern with a real lit candle inside and singing
special songs with my nanny and aunts.

And at the end of the month comes the Small Bairam.
So the last few days are dedicated to cake-making. My
grandmother and the women of the family sit around on
the floor in a circle, chatting. Between their legs they hold
the large copper urns and in them they knead the dough

for the cakes. They roll the dough into little balls and stuff each one with some dates. Then they flatten them and lay them on huge black oven trays. Each cake has to have a pattern engraved on it with special pincers, and this is where I join in. I crawl around the trays making patterns with my silver pincers. On a few I am allowed to draw faces. When the cakes are all done, the servants balance the huge black trays on their heads and carry them to the public oven.

For the Bairam you always wear new clothes. They are specially made and on the Eve of the feast they are laid out ready to be worn in the morning. The Big Bairam lasts four days. Weeks before it, Grandfather buys a sheep and it is tethered to the iron railings on the balcony. Going to my grandfather's house becomes extra special: there is the sheep to ride and play with. But then, on the Eve of the Bairam, they tell me to say goodbye to the sheep. They tell me he is going back to his mother. He has enjoyed playing with me but now it is time for him to go home. I go to sleep in a huge bed with springs and a feather quilt and when I wake up he has gone. I miss him. But I agree: a sheep should be with his mother. And I am consoled by the new clothes and by the fireworks they buy me. Catherine wheels make brilliant arcs of light, torpedoes go off with a deafening blast, Italian War catches fire in your hand when you scrape it against the wall (only the wall of the back staircase, nowhere else), and sparklers throw off a breathtaking profusion of stars and moons. This is the Bairam.

Another main event in life is the yearly migration to Alexandria. In July the whole family packs beachwear and bundles into cars and we set off on the long desert road to the Mediterranean. In Alexandria there is a two-storey wooden house standing in an acre of sandy ground with palm trees. This is the 'chalet'. It is where I live during July and August. It is a short walk to the beach and we stroll it in our swimwear. On the beach they set up brilliant parasols and deck-chairs and rugs. My aunts teach me to swim. My father and uncle throw me to each other in the water, occasionally dousing me in the surf. On the days when my grandfather comes up from Cairo he teaches me to play backgammon on an intricate, inlaid board. He teaches me the classic manoeuvres and the set moves. And he gives me silver money when I beat him.

To everything there is an order and a pattern.

Parental decree forbids servants and relatives to tell frightening stories or threaten abduction by the Ghoul or the Bogey or the Man with the Skinned Leg. So I grow up in ignorance of the more menacing figures of folklore. I know Cinderella well, and am repeatedly ecstatic as the glass slipper is fitted to her dainty foot; I have unbounded confidence in Clever Hassan who always comes out on top; and I know that the real story of Little Red Riding Hood ends with her and her grandmother emerging triumphantly from the wolf's belly. The wolf is so overcome by this miracle that he is transformed into a domestic pet and they all live together happily ever after.

Divine Order. Evil is a passing naughtiness; mighty forces work for the good and all stories end happily.

Knowing

I endlessly make up tales surrounding the pictures in the books I cannot yet read. I pore over a bookful of Rodin sculptures and my parents are delighted with the sunny little fables I produce. My life is woven into my tales and my tales become part of my life: aunts and uncles are characters in a storybook and Hansel and Gretel join me under the desk in my grandfather's shop. I invent characters who become my friends and perform a play with them to an assembled family audience. 'The child has such a lively imagination,' they say, and surround me with admiration and love.

My parents' books become increasingly fascinating. I pick up even the ones with sparse illustrations and ask questions: 'Who is this?'

'A man called Vathek.'

'Where does he live?'

'He's not real. He was invented by a man called Beckford.'

'Where does *he* live?'

'He lived in the last century, in England.'

My father's books are still out of bounds.

Then there comes a break. My mother is absent for months and I live in the Spoiling-House. Then I go on a long journey across the sea alone with my father. My first train. A cold, dark, wet, windy place with a lot of people and a lot of trains. My father and I sit in a café drinking hot milk. Then my mother's face emerges out of the rain. She is wearing a light green raincoat. She runs into my father's arms and I embrace her legs. She

75

bends to pick me up and she is laughing and crying at the same time.

Now I remember a new home. It is much smaller than the ones we've left behind and not so pretty. But there is a fire in the living-room wall. Everything here is much colder, much darker than I'm used to. No one. No one except my parents. And I don't see very much of *them*, for I am sent to school. My parents are pleased that I find my feet and learn the new language so easily. I miss my aunts and uncles and grandparents. But now I like my new friends. I like sitting on the floor on a huge sheet of paper and painting grey castles and soldiers in red and black uniforms. I like cuddling up to Miss Eve at storytime. I like taking a goldfish home for the holidays. I miss the sun. But I like the evenings when I sit at my mother's feet in front of the fire. She reads and writes and I look at pictures. There are no sugar dolls, no Ramadan lantern, no Bairam and no sheep. But instead there is Father Christmas and a stockingful of presents.

A new routine is introduced, I am initiated into a semi-grown-up role. Once a week my parents go out in the evening and I am left on my own. My mother gives me my bath and my dinner, then tucks me up in bed with a hot-water bottle. Both my mother and father kiss me goodnight. A small nightlight is left burning. I don't mind at all. I tell myself stories till I fall asleep. In the morning the Brownie will have visited me and left a chocolate or a packet of sweets under my pillow. He always comes when my parents go out in the evening. He never forgets. I try to wait up for him but I always fall asleep.

One night after I've fallen asleep I am suddenly wide awake. I sit up in bed and there, by the wall, I see him. He is a cross between a tiny man and a hamster. He is running quickly, upright on two legs and he wears a little green suit and hat. He has a human face with a black mouse snout and pointed pixie ears. I know instantly that it's the Brownie and I sit very still so as not to frighten him away. Then I wonder about his gift. I slip my hand under the pillow but there's nothing there. I twist around to look and make sure. Still nothing. When I look up, he has gone. I know he will be back with my present so I sit up to wait for him. The next thing I know it is morning and my mother is waking me up. There is a bag of liquorice under the pillow. Over cornflakes I tell my parents that I've seen the Brownie. At first they smile, then, as I describe the scene in detail they start to look anxious.

'You couldn't have, dear.'

'But I did.'

'You must have dreamt it.'

'But I was *sitting up* in bed. I wasn't asleep.'

'You couldn't *really* have seen the Brownie.'

'Why?'

'Because . . . Well, because he can only come when you're asleep.'

'But I *was* asleep. Then I woke up and he ran away.'

They stop arguing with me but they still look uncomfortable and I cannot understand why.

An important event now takes place: I learn to read. One day, all of a sudden, the black marks around the pictures make sense and I am reading. Now, every day on the way home from school, we stop at the public library and get me a book. Also, once a week, I buy *Playhour* and *Robin*. I want to do nothing but read. I read and I read and I make up more stories. I go right through *Little Grey Rabbit* and *Noddy* and Hans Christian Andersen and my world is peopled with fascinating characters and bursting with adventure. Pinocchio and Squirrel go with me everywhere. I take to saving up my pocket money and buying comics. The Brownie stops bringing me sweets and brings me books instead. Every book is a treasure trove and I play a part in every story.

One week I go to get my *Playhour* and am attracted by another comic. The cover shows a man in a black cloak and a beautiful blonde lady. The lady is tired so he is carrying her and smiling. He has horrid teeth. Over the picture is written *Vampires*. I don't know what that means but I already have a penchant for the romantic. I buy it. Something tells me my parents won't approve so I smuggle it in and hide it among my toys till their next going-out night.

This time, not only don't I mind: I positively *want* them to go. When they do, I sit up in bed and read by the nightlight: 'The undead ... those monstrous characters who feed upon the blood of the living ... In Transylvania, Count Dracula's castle lay shrouded in blackest night ...' Here is new material indeed for my imagination. That night (after carefully rehiding the comic), I have a nightmare. An octopus is trying to catch me to drive a stake through my heart. I can see my mother but she cannot see me or hear me scream. Luckily, my parents have come home. They wake me up and comfort me and I tell them about the octopus but not about the stake. My father tells me that if I am afraid I'll dream of something, the thing to do is to remember it consciously before I go to sleep. Then I won't dream of it. For nights afterwards I religiously intone 'Octopuses and Vampires, Octopuses and Vampires' before I go to sleep. It works. I don't dream of them. I also don't buy any more Vampire comics.

My mother has a problem with me. I am finishing my books too quickly. We get home from school and long before bed-time I have finished the books from the library and am demanding more. In desperation she lets me browse among her books. I pick out a heavy red and gold volume of the *Arabian Nights*. 'It's all right,' she assures my father, 'it's only the Lane edition.' And I enter yet another new world. A world of Oriental souks and magic and Djinnis. I am fascinated by the way Djinnis can emerge from lamps, bottles, jars, in fact from anything. The world has undreamt-of possibilities. During the day I am at school and in the evening I am sunk completely into this fire-lit world of magic.

The week rolls round and it is going-out night again. I have my bath and my chicken soup and get into bed. My parents tuck me in and kiss me. I lie on my side in bed, gazing at the wall. The nightlight is burning. Slowly, slowly, the wall begins to move. I stare at it. It splits down the middle and swings slowly and silently open. In front of my eyes appears a giant black Djinni with a shaved head. All he wears is a Tarzan-like swimsuit in leopard-skin, and his bulging arms are folded across his bare chest. Behind him appears the Vampire in the black cloak. He is grinning widely and his long teeth are dripping with blood. For long seconds I am mesmerised, then I unfreeze. In a flash I am out of bed and on the chest of drawers under the window.

My parents are still in the courtyard when they hear the sound of banging against glass. They turn and look up. A small figure in a white nightdress performs a demented dance behind the darkened window-panes. Fists hitting at the glass, mouth wide open in a silent scream. They race back up the stairs, unlock the door and rush in. I am still on the chest beneath the window as, hysterical, I explain what happened. They tell me it cannot be and try to laugh at me. But whatever they tell me is no use for it *has* been and I have seen it. They are not able to explain it away.

My father sits in the living-room and my mother comes and goes between us.

'I must go down now and you must go back to bed.'

'No.' I am hysterical and crying.

'Daddy says he'll be very cross with you.'

'. . .'

'Daddy says there won't be any new toys or books till Christmas.'

'I don't want any.'

I know now my parents are neither omnipotent

nor omniscient. They cannot stop the Vampire from appearing but at least they can be there when he arrives. I insist that they stay in and I win. I will never be left alone after this. And I am miserable.

The Wedding of Zeina

'I was fifteen,' Zeina began. 'He was nineteen and already doing well. He was a butcher like his father and worked with him. One day my grandmother came and called me. She took me to one side and said,

'"Zeina, you're going to marry Sobhi."

'"But, Setti, how do I marry him?" I asked.

'He was my cousin: the son of my dead mother's sister, but I knew nothing of marriage.

'"You'll be his wife and he'll be your husband and you'll serve him and do what he tells you."

'I started to cry.

'"Will I have to leave you, Setti?"

'The old woman took me in her arms:

'"No, no, you'll have your own room in the house and I'll always be with you. You're a big girl now. You can cook and clean and look after a man and he's your cousin, child, he's not a stranger."

'Well . . . I went out to the other girls in the yard but my heart was full of my new importance. I didn't say anything but in a few hours everyone knew anyway and Sobhi stopped coming to our part of the house. From the time Setti told me, I only saw him again on the wedding night.'

The sound of a bicycle bell rang through the darkness and Zeina refolded her legs and settled more comfortably against the banisters.

'My bridal box had been ready for years and my uncle arranged for the painters to come and decorate a room on the roof of the house. It had a little bathroom next to it with a toilet, a basin and a shower and I was to cook in the big kitchen downstairs with my grandmother and aunt. They painted the room a very pretty pink and we put in a red rug and a bed and a cupboard and a chair and a little mirror.'

The little girl listening smiled. It sounded lovely. Her grandfather's house had a room on the roof. They kept rabbits there and she was allowed sometimes to go up and play with them. They were all different colours –

'When the day before the wedding came the younger children were all put out into the yard and the Mashta was sent for –'

'Mashta?'

'Yes, she's the woman who comes to adorn the bride. They fetched her from the baths and she hurried in, trilling her joy-cries from the top of the street. "A thousand congratulations, Zeina," she cried, letting out another joy-cry before she took off her *tarha* and hugged me, kissing me on the mouth. I clung closer to my grandmother. "They say he's a fine young man," she said, laughing, and pinched me, then she took off her slippers and her outer black dress, rolled up her sleeves and went into the kitchen to prepare the candy. I had seen the older women use it before –'

'Candy?'

'It's what you take out your hair with.'

'Why would you take out your hair?' the little girl wondered, gazing at her nurse's rich head of shiny black hair. Dada Zeina usually wore it bundled under a white kerchief like all the other nannies in the club, but tonight was Wednesday and it had been washed in olive-oil soap and was drying round her shoulders. That too was part of the magic of these nights.

'The hair on your legs and your body, to make you nice and smooth for the bridegroom.'

Her nurse looked at her meaningfully and the child thrilled. Here she was: an accomplice, a grown-up. Her baby sister and brother were asleep inside, but she was eight years old and sitting up on the balcony listening to her nanny's story. And it would be like this every Wednesday night when her parents went out. So long, of course, as she was careful and kept the secret. 'She's a good girl,' Dada Zeina always said to the other nurses in the club, 'she never carries tales to her mother.' And although in some deep corner inside she was uneasy, feeling the bribe in the words, she still felt proud, and anxious to keep those privileged story-telling hours. Besides, she didn't want to carry tales. She had asked her mother once how women did the joy-cry and her father had frowned and said it was something that only vulgar people did.

'They told me to undress and I was so shy,' said Zeina, laughing. 'I held on to my grandmother, but she pulled up my shift and my aunt took it off me, and my undershift too, and sat me down on the straw mat. The Mashta was kneading the candy in her hands and as it crackled and popped she'd say, 'Listen to that. How he must love her if the candy's popping like this. What a lucky girl you are!" and let out another joy-cry. She smoothed the paste on to my leg, muttered the name of God and tore it off. I howled and jumped up but they pulled me down again:

"'Don't be a child, now."

"'Your body will go numb in a moment and you won't feel the pain."

"'It's all so you can please your man."

"'What's he got to do with my legs?" I cried. I was so foolish.'

Zeina laughed.

The little girl noticed then the soft down on her own arms and legs but, anxious to stay a grown-up, she laughed too.

'Well, they plucked my legs and thighs and armpits and arms and my face too, for good measure, then the Mashta said, "Come on, bride, take your knickers off," and I was so startled I cringed into myself and couldn't move.'

The little girl sat very still. She had the strangest, warmest, gentlest, tingling feeling between her legs and her heart was pounding in both fear and pleasure. This was forbidden. Her parents never ever said 'knickers', always 'culottes' and her nurse, in deference to then, said 'kollott' but now, now she was using the other, the 'vulgar' word.

"'Come on, Zeina, don't be a spoilt child," my aunt said, and tugged my knickers off. They spread the paste on the hair –'

What hair? wondered the child but she would not stop the flow for anything now.

'– and pulled. It was fire. I tried to struggle up but they held me down and the Mashta went on spreading the paste and tearing it off while I cried and screamed until I was completely clean. Then they heated water and poured it into the large brass tub and I sat in it stark naked while the Mashta rubbed me all over with a rough cloth, trilling her joy-cries all the while. Then she dried me and my grandmother fetched me a clean shift and sent me to lie down and rest.'

Aisha was quiet. 'We ought to go to bed before your parents come back,' said her nanny. 'Oh no,' eyes enormous, 'they're at the ballet. They won't be back before twelve at least. Please, *please* go on. What happened next?'

'Next day they brought up a hundred chairs to the roof. The neighbours came and helped with the cooking and we cleaned out the room and the bathroom.'

'Was your room on the roof like my grandfather's?'

'What?'

'Where they keep the rabbits.'

'What rabbits?'

'Oh Dada, you know, on top of my grandfather's house, where the *rabbits* are.'

'Oh. Yes, well, but it was clean and pink and had furniture –'

Rabbits didn't need furniture but perhaps they would like pink walls. Perhaps if she persuaded her grandfather they would be happier, he would have the walls painted pink? But maybe grown-ups didn't really care about rabbits being happy. A treacherous wave of misery hit her as she remembered playing with the rabbits one day when her nurse casually caught one of them. She held him by the ears and he hung and quivered, huge eyes rolled back. When she slit his throat the blood spurted and he kicked and danced around before finally going limp, defeated. She had hated Dada Zeina then.

'I had a beautiful dress with sequins and a pink veil and I forgot about being a bride and sat and laughed with my girlfriends. But Setti came and took me away and took me to my uncle. My uncles were butchers and they're very tough men. My uncle had a gun in one hand and he held me by the other. I was scared of the gun because I'd heard of some girl they'd shot on her wedding night, but he led me to the new room. My aunt was there and my grandmother came in. Then the bridegroom came, my cousin. He had a thick white bandage wrapped round the middle finger of his right hand and I thought he had hurt it. I was so foolish. My uncle said, 'I'll be right outside,' and closed the door but I could still hear the drums and flutes as loud as though they were in the room with us. My aunt put her hand on my shoulder and said, "Take off your knickers, child, and lie down on the rug." I stared at her without understanding. She shook me a little: "Come on, girl, your uncles are waiting." I still stood there. "Tell him to get out," I said pointing at the man.

'"The girl is mad," said my aunt.

'"He's your husband," said my grandmother gently.

'"I won't undress in front of him," I said.

'My aunt suddenly tried to pull me to the floor but

I fought her. *He* just stood watching with his finger in the bandage. My aunt opened the door and went out. I could hear my uncle's voice raised angrily, then my aunt came back in with two women.

'"The girl is hard-headed," said one.

'"She's still young and foolish," said my grandmother. "Don't scare her lest blood should disappear."

'Suddenly the four women surrounded me and pulled me to the floor. One pinned down my shoulders while the other held on to my waist and my aunt and grandmother pulled off my knickers. I struggled and clamped my legs together tight. My aunt was pinching my thighs, trying to get me to open up. I was yelling and screaming but I kept my thighs tight together. My uncle hammered on the door: "What the Hell's going on in there? Curse you all. Shall I come in and shoot the bitch?" "It's all right, brother, have patience," cried my aunt and bent down suddenly and bit my upper thigh so hard I jerked it away and they immediately pulled my legs apart and held them and *he* stepped forward and squatted between them. I managed to wrench a leg away and as he leaned forward I gave him a mighty kick that sent him sprawling on his backside. He looked so funny sitting there on his bum, surprised, then he jumped up and came at me and slapped my face, then using all his man's strength he forced my thighs open, threaded one of my arms behind each knee and drew them up to my head. The women held my arms and I lay there squirming and crying in gasps as he knelt down and forced his bandaged finger into me, working it round and round and in and out as I screamed and screamed. Finally he took it out. The bandage was soaked with blood. They let go of me and Setti drew my wedding dress down and I lay shivering and crying. Then he went out. I heard my uncle fire his gun into the air and my other uncles' guns answering it from around the house and the street. Then the drumming went up very loud and the joy-cries filled the air and through the door I could see them unwrapping the bandage from around his finger. My uncle wound it round his head, blood and all, and danced slowly and proudly into the crowd, using his gun like a cane to dance with and calling out, "Our Honour, Our daughter's Honour, Our family's Honour."

'Afterwards Setti explained that he was my husband and any time he wanted to do anything with me I must let him and not fight him. But I did,' Zeina said, laughing. 'I fought him every time for a month, but in the end he mastered me.'

'Did you hate him, Dada?' the child asked gently.

Zeina laughed again, easily. 'No, of course not. He was a strong man, bless him. And besides he was as big as a bull.'

Her Man

Zeina sat on the bed in her room on the roof, staring out of the window. The sun had set but there was still some light left in the pale blue sky. Clouds were gathering and she could see the clothes hanging out to dry on the neighbours' rooftop blowing in the rising wind. It was time to call Sa'd in from the street and give him his supper. She sighed. What bent luck, Zeina, she thought. Young and full of youth and pretty, with eyelashes black as night even without kohl and a face fair and full of light and hair smooth as silk. What thighs. What legs. The men are always looking at them as you walk down the street, your *melaya* draped tightly round your body but showing one full, straight leg with a dimpled ankle adorned by a thick silver anklet. Like that boy, what's his name, the greengrocer's apprentice, ogling you till you had to chide him. 'What's wrong with you, boy? You've never seen a woman before?' And he – curse his cheek – he said, 'I've seen women, Set Om Sa'd, but by the life of Seedna Mohammad, the Prophet, I've never seen one with legs like yours.' A crazy boy. Of course you told him off, drawing your *melaya* across your face to hide your smile, 'Shut up, boy. You must be mad, or something's gone wrong with your head. Don't you know what my husband would do to you if he knew what you said? Haven't you heard that his anger is worse than that of Iblis, the Devil?'

My husband. She sighed again, her hand restless on her thigh. Life without a man was worth nothing. It was no life at all. The days were long and heavy now that she had no man to look after, to cook for, to clean and adorn herself for. And at night she fell, alone, into a thick, dense sleep from which there was no urgent hand to wake her. Pull yourself together, now, Zeina, she told herself, and go and get your son from the lane. All the other children must have gone home by now. Go.

She got up slowly and walked out of the room, closing the door carefully behind her. The wind was getting really strong now, blowing her shift as she walked across the roof and to the door leading into the heart of the building. She walked down the dark, familiar stairs, past her sister's quarters and her aunt's and grandmother's quarters, and out into the street. The wind was whipping up clouds of dust which blew into her mouth and eyes as she looked for her son. 'Sa'd,' she called, 'Sa'd, where are you, boy?' She saw him at last at the end of the lane, in a doorway, sheltering from the wind. He came running as she called and held tightly on to her hand as they walked up the lane and back to the house. 'I was scared of the wind,' he complained. She felt a surge of tenderness. He was nine years old. Born just one year after her marriage. The girl that had followed him two years later God had seen fit to take away and there had been as yet no others. And now, perhaps there never would be.

And yet one never knew how things would turn out. Faith, faith, Zeina, she reminded herself. Have faith in God and it will all turn out to the good. She took Sa'd into the large kitchen where his cousins, her sister's two sons, were already eating. He joined them on the floor at the low, round, wooden table, taking possession of a loaf and dipping his bread into the large bowl of stew in the middle. The men were out for the evening and her sister and grandmother sat on the mat at the far end of the kitchen, drinking coffee. Zeina walked over and sat down by her grandmother, folding her legs.

'Well, he should be back tomorrow,' said Hekmat, her sister, immediately.

'Who should be back tomorrow?' Zeina asked blandly.

'Who should it be? The Djinn? Sobhi, your husband, woman.'

'Oh.'

'What d'you mean, "oh"? Aren't you happy he's coming back?'

'What's it to do with me?'

'What's it to do with you? How can you say that? Isn't he your husband?' Then, as she understood, 'You're not going on with that game you're playing, are you? Setti,' turning to the old woman, 'see what this madwoman here is thinking of. The man's been away for ten days and he'll come back to find his wife not speaking to him. Does this make sense?'

'Let his other wife speak to him,' said Zeina before her grandmother could answer.

'Why, of course she'll speak to him,' began her sister, 'and not only will she speak to him –'

'That's what we're afraid of, child,' cut in the old woman, carefully swirling the coffee dregs around and upturning the cup on its saucer. 'If you keep away from him long enough he'll grow used to being without you and cleave to her completely. What will you do then?'

'Kick yourself,' supplied Hekmat. 'Beat yourself with a slipper, most likely, and then he won't care.'

'Remember the proverb, child: the shade of a man is better than that of a wall. And he hasn't done anything that other men don't do. He's still your husband. He hasn't left you or neglected you. He still supports you and brings you meat and fruit, even though you've not been speaking to him. He still holds you dear. But you're hurting his pride and his manhood. Take care what you're doing lest you drive him away.'

'Drive him away?' cried Zeina bitterly. 'How can I drive him further away than he's already gone? To marry on top of me? Why? Am I old? Or has my hair gone white? Or am I ugly? Or have my teeth fallen out? Or don't I please him any more? Or am I not a good housewife? Haven't I borne him a son and a daughter, may God have mercy on her? What is wrong with me that he should marry on top of me?'

'There's nothing wrong with you, child, and a thousand men would desire you. But these things are in the hands of God. Doesn't the Koran say "And you may hate that very thing which is best for you?" You know Sobhi's always been impulsive. He acts first and regrets later, and if he's not already regretting this, he will in a while.'

'The girl's a dope,' said Hekmat. 'Why, she can't even

98

put two words together and she's always staring as if she's in a daze. He'll soon get bored with her.'

'Maybe he does not want her to talk to him,' said Zeina. 'Maybe the other's enough for him –'

'How d'you know she's good at the other?' asked her sister. 'She's not even carrying yet. I know because before she went to her mother's I saw her washing out her curse cloths, so she's not carrying and she's already been married four months.'

'Has it been four months?' asked the old woman. 'So it's already been six months since Sheikh Mahgoub died. Eh, the days pass and life runs by. The train waits for no one. Sobhi thought he was doing right marrying the girl when her father died. God commanded us to protect our neighbours' honour and the girl has no brothers, no uncles, no menfolk. He preserved Sheikh Mahgoub's honour by marrying Tahiyya.'

'Preserved Sheikh Mahgoub's honour?' broke in Zeina sharply. 'He had the hots for her, that's all. He's always had a roving eye and he likes women. He was randy for her. And her mother wasn't asking a bride-price. Who would pay a bride-price for a half-idiot orphan? He got her cheap. All he had to do was find her somewhere to live, so he took Sa'd's room – right next to mind, mind you – and sent him to sleep with me. Well, of course, why should he want me alone in the room now? He used to be anxious enough to send the boy to the other room, but that was in the old days –'

'Come on, Zeina,' said her sister. 'You know Sa'd sleeps down here with his cousins most of the time.' Then, remembering the children, she turned to them sharply. 'What are you doing here? Sitting listening? You've finished eating so get off to your room and play there.' She faced back to her sister. 'You know something? I think Sobhi put her in the room next to you so you could keep an eye on her. He knew you'd watch her like a hawk and make sure he heard if she got up to anything she shouldn't.'

'Up to anything? I tell you, the girl's an idiot. She wouldn't even know how to go about it. And why should she? She's got herself a man of her own. If she wanted to play around she could have done it now. He's been away at this funeral for ten days. But instead she chooses to go and stay with her mother.'

'The girl's very young,' put in the grandmother. 'She said she was afraid to sleep on her own on the roof. Maybe she's a bit scared of you as well –'

'Scared of *me*? Why should she be scared of me? What have I done to scare her? I haven't come near her from the day she moved in here.'

'That's because you're thick,' interrupted Hekmat. 'Another woman would have found means of getting rid of her.'

'So what should I do? Play tricks on her? Pour salt into her cooking? Cut up her clothes? Sprinkle dust in her room? And when she complains to him? What would happen then? You know what he's like when he's angry: he doesn't stop to ask questions. Right now she's the apple of his eye. He'd just fly into a rage and God knows what he'd do to me.'

'You've always been wise, Zeina,' said her grandmother approvingly. 'Wise and careful. It's true. It would do you no good to anger him now. Better to wait and see what God will bring to pass.'

Hekmat suddenly laughed. 'You must miss him, though,' she said, leaning forward and gently pinching her sister's breast. 'Remember how you always used to tell us how much he pleased you? "My man," you'd say proudly, "my man is as big as a bull and knows how to make a woman happy." Well, it can't be easy now that you're not even speaking to him, hey?' She laughed loudly.

'For shame, Hekmat,' said her grandmother, gazing at the patterns in the coffee cup, 'the children will hear you. Don't you know that a well-bred woman can do without a man even for six months?'

There was a sound behind them and Hekmat turned, still laughing, to the door. Her expression changed as she caught sight of the girl standing there. 'Oh Lord,' she cried in exaggerated surprise, 'look who's come in. Well, *you've* given me a fright,' pulling her neckline out and pretending to spit in her bosom. 'The man doesn't come back till tomorrow. What brings *you* back tonight? Is your mother bored with you or didn't she want to feed you any more? Not that you eat much anyway, being as skinny as you are –'

Tahiyya stepped sideways from the door into the kitchen. She stood by the wall, still clutching her *melaya* round her, her hand clenched tightly upon the neck of a bundle that she held. She spoke like one in a dream. 'The wind is very high outside. Can't you hear it? The air in the street is so full of dust that you can't see a hand's length in front of your eyes.' Then she remembered.

'Good evening, Setti,' moving forward to kiss the old woman's hand. 'My mother salutes you and she's sent you some cakes she made just this morning.' She offered the bundle to the old woman who took it from her saying kindly, 'And why go to all this trouble, daughter? Is your mother well?'

'She's well, praise God, and asks after your health.'

'I'm well, praise God. As well as can be expected for an old woman like me.'

'May God lengthen your life and give you good health,' responded the three younger women in a chorus. It was the only time Zeina spoke.

'You haven't told us why you've come back,' insisted Hekmat, staring at the girl, her hands on her waist.

'My mother said I should. She said it would give me an early start tomorrow in cleaning the room and preparing for Si Sobhi's coming back. I didn't want to come because of the wind but she said I should.'

'You're scared of the wind?' asked Hekmat contemptuously. She got up suddenly so that Tahiyya flinched and retreated to the door. But Hekmat walked past her and to the corner where the table stood. She began clearing up the remnants of the boys' supper. 'Scared of the wind,' she repeated, mimicking the girl's timid manner, 'scared of the wind and scared of the dark and scared to sleep on her own on the roof. What a coward. How come you're not scared of the man? Or doesn't that,' wiggling a finger in the girl's face in an obscene gesture, 'scare you?'

'Stop it, Hekmat,' said the grandmother. 'Leave the girl alone.' She looked across at Zeina but she just sat there impassively. 'Tahiyya, have you had any dinner, child, or shall I put some out for you? There's a bit of stew left over from the boys. Do you want to heat it?'

Zeina stood up suddenly. 'I'm going up to my room,' she said. 'Sa'd,' she raised her voice, 'Sa'd, come along. We're going up.'

The little boy ran into the room: 'I want to sleep down here tonight. We're playing.'

Zeina looked at her sister.

'Leave the boy,' said Hekmat. 'He's no trouble to anyone. Wherever he lays his head he sleeps.'

'You're not to be naughty,' Zeina warned her son. 'If your aunt complains of you I'll give you a beating –' but he had already turned and run back into the bedroom with his cousins.

Zeina said a vague 'goodnight' and climbed slowly to the roof. The wind was howling and she held her clothes down with both hands, lowering her head as she ran for her room. She pushed the door shut against the wind and stood leaning against it. Why had he married her? Why? She was young, yes, but then she, Zeina, was not old. Twenty-five was not old. And she wasn't any prettier than her. And she was simple. Why did he want to marry a simpleton? She lit the paraffin lamp and took her towel from the nail behind the door and went out again into the wind, taking the lamp with her. She ran into the bathroom and shut the door. She put the lamp on the floor and started washing herself with cold water. Things had been good between them. Never mind the odd quarrel. Everybody quarrelled sometimes. And she had done everything for him that a woman could do for a man. She had been so young when she married him:

only fifteen and knowing nothing of marriage. But she had learnt fast and he always said she pleased him. Why then did he have to go and marry a young, half-baked idiot who wouldn't know the first thing about pleasing a man? She'd have understood it more if the girl had been crafty. If she had laid snares for him. But she was simple. What was it he saw in her?

She let herself out and went back to her room. The shutters were knocking against the wall as the wind blew them and she opened the window and pulled them to, closing the window again carefully. She pulled back the blanket, blew out the lamp and got into bed. What bent luck, Zeina, she thought. Young and full of youth and beautiful, and you have to go to bed without your man. Tomorrow he's coming back, she thought. But what's the use? He's coming back to her, not to me. Her mind dwelt on tomorrow. He would come back, probably with a gift of fruit. He would appear at the doorway to the roof and walk towards the room. Which room? Hers? Tahiyya's? The images were mixed in her mind. 'Hey, girl,' he'd shout and she would come running out and take the fruit and his bundle of clothes from him and follow him into the room. 'Praise God that you've come home safely, Abu Sa'd,' she'd say and he would thank her and enquire after her health. She would ask if he wanted to wash and would hand him the towel and he would turn and go into the bathroom, where he'd wash the dust of the journey from his face and his hands. Then he would come back to the room, still drying his hands, and give her back the towel. As she hung it up he would approach her from behind, putting his arms around her and his hands on her breasts. She would pretend to be embarrassed and pull away, saying shyly, 'Don't you want to eat?' and he would laugh, showing his strong, tobacco-stained teeth and say, 'What's the matter, girl? Haven't you missed me?' and he would take her by the arm and sit her down on the bed. Zeina's hand was between her legs as she drifted into a heavy sleep.

Tahiyya came slowly up the stairs. She hesitated at the doorway, gathering her courage for the dash across the dark, windy roof. Then, holding her clothes down, she ran across and straight into the bathroom. She washed herself carefully and ritually performed her ablutions. She did not wash her hair but passed her wet hand thrice over it. Then, dripping water, she ran into her room.

The room felt cold and lonely. She had been away for ten days and although she knew this was now her home, she felt herself a stranger. She took her towel off the nail on the wall and dried herself, then she lit the paraffin lamp and laid out her prayer rug. She covered her head with the white head-dress and stood on the rug, going through her evening prayers. She made the obeisances and said the farewells, then sat back on her heels, passing her hands over her face in a habit learnt from watching her father pray over the years. She continued for a while to sit on the prayer mat, drawing a faint comfort from the familiar gestures. But the wind howled and the lamp made the shadows dance in the corners and her room had no key and no bolt.

As she slept, Zeina felt a hand move gently, tentatively over her back. An edge of consciousness came into her sleep. It was not a familiar touch. Sobhi's hands were never tentative. But it was pleasant and blended into her dream as she drifted again into sleep. The covers were lifted and a cold body huddled, trembling, against her back. 'Please, Om Sa'd,' Tahiyya's voice whispered, 'my room is cold and the wind is so loud and there's knocking everywhere and I'm so scared.' She shook with tears.

Zeina turned, half asleep, and put her arms round the trembling girl. 'All right, all right, hush it's all right.' Tahiyya clung to her, shivering and Zeina sleepily rubbed her body, trying vaguely to warm her. Her hands moved over Tahiyya's back and her breasts and belly then lower down as she rubbed her thighs. The girl clung to her. She smelt of soap and her breath was clean and fresh. Zeina went on rubbing her thighs. Tahiyya's hands, still shivering, began to stroke her back. Her hands felt soft and gentle. Hardly conscious, Zeina enjoyed the long-missed tingling flowing down her spine. Tahiyya's hands were naïve as they stroked the older woman and her own body was moving and arching under Zeina's touch. Her touch was strangely like Sobhi's, her hands did the same things, pressed in the same ways and Tahiyya's body answered. Zeina felt the pliant body move under her hands. Her hand found its way to Tahiyya's neckline and, drawing it down, fingered the girl's naked breast. Tahiyya's hands clutched at her back. A feeling of power surged through her. Gently she pinched the nipple and heard the girl gasp. She went on pressing. Tahiyya was writhing, pressing her body against hers. On an impulse she took her hand from her breast, passed it down the front of the girl's body then dug it hard, taking the shift with it, between her legs. Tahiyya caught her breath, then let it out with a sob. Zeina was wide awake now, staring in the dark at the moving body she held in her arms. Tahiyya's eyes were closed, her mouth half open and her forehead gleamed with sweat. So this was what she was like. This was what she was like with him. This was what he now found waiting in bed for him every night. It must make him feel really proud. Make him feel like the master of men. Zeina stopped stroking and pinched the inside of Tahiyya's thigh hard. The girl only moaned and shifted slightly, opening her legs. Then Zeina had her idea. She bent over the girl's body, lifted her dress and started to lick her thighs.

Tahiyya twisted under her tongue. Zeina worked slowly, now with the flat of her tongue, now drawing lines and circles with its tip. She moved up and started nibbling gently at her buttocks while her hand moved expertly between Tahiyya's open thighs. The girl was whimpering, crying, now for her mother, now for Seedna Mohammad, as Zeina found her most sensitive spots and manipulated them carefully. Zeina waited, fingers busy, teeth working, until Tahiyya's whimperings grew incoherent and she started to moan and convulse. Then she dug her teeth sharply into her right buttock. The bite seemed to heighten the girl's pleasure for she crashed around crying out and Zeina kept her teeth in and sucked hard. Then, as the waves receded, she gave up the mouthful of flesh and drew the girl's dress down over her thighs. She sat up in the dark. 'You liked that?' 'May God bring it to a good end,' sobbed Tahiyya.

In the morning the wind had died down and the winter sun shone white in a cloudless blue sky. Zeina

107

went downstairs and woke her son. She gave him his breakfast of beans and bread and saw him off to school, then collected the broom, dustpan, a metal pail and a floorcloth and climbed back to the roof. She opened the door of her room. Her bed was empty. She went in, rolled up the rug and took it out on to the roof and shook it. Then she started to clean her room thoroughly, washing the floor and polishing the window and the mirror. She made the bed with fresh sheets and hung a clean towel on the nail behind the door. When she had finished, she went in and scrubbed out the bathroom, then she lit the Primus and put a large pot of water over it. She stood at the door of the bathroom looking out across the roof. Tahiyya came out of her room and stood in the doorway, feeling the sun on her feet. On her face was a quiet, abstracted smile. Zeina waited. When the girl showed no sign of moving, she snapped, 'You'd better get moving if you're going to go to the market and come back in time to cook his dinner.' Tahiyya disappeared into the room and returned with her slippers and *melaya* on. She made for the stairs.

The water was hot. Zeina poured it into the copper tub, then stripped and bathed herself carefully. She took her time washing her long black hair, then, sitting in the sun, she combed it out, parting it in the middle and braiding it into two thick plaits which she twisted round her head.

When Sa'd came home from school, Zeina took him downstairs and fed him. Afterwards, she sent him out to play in the street. On her way back up she stopped at her sister's quarters. 'Let Sa'd sleep with his cousins tonight, will you?' 'Naturally,' said Hekmat, jiggling her eyebrows with a broad smile.

Zeina went upstairs and into her room. She stood in the middle of the room for a moment, then crossed over to the cupboard and took out her kohl vial and a small bottle of scent. She opened the bottle and sniffed the heavy fragrance, then she closed it again and went over to the mirror and looked in it carefully. There wasn't a blemish on her face; her brow was smooth, her hair was black as night. She looked over her shoulder at her hips and legs. They were nice and plump and firm. A sea for a man to drown in. What more did he want? She took the scent and the kohl back to the cupboard. She went out on to the roof and chose a sunny spot from where she could see the door. Then she sat cross-legged on the tiled floor and waited.

In a while she heard Tahiyya coming up. The girl was not wearing her *melaya* and slippers. She was carrying them under her arm.

'You've been to market?'

'I came back long ago. I've been in the kitchen. I've cooked a great meal of okra with lamb and made some rice to go with it.'

'Good.'

Tahiyya was willing to stay and chat but Zeina looked resolutely into the distance, so she went into her room. She was strange, Zeina. She hadn't behaved as Tahiyya had been warned a first wife would. She had expected fights and beatings, her few shifts to be torn to shreds and her cooking systematically ruined with vinegar or salt. But none of that had happened. And then last night

Zeina had been kind to her. Last night – well, Sobhi would be here soon and she had to get ready for him. She started cleaning her room.

Tahiyya was heating the water for her husband's bath. She was pumping the Primus to go full blast so she did not hear Zeina call softly, 'Abu Sa'd, I want a word with you.' The man followed Zeina into her room. Large, but graceful in his blue woollen *galabiya* and leather slippers, his cane and a bundle of clothes in one hand and under his arm a large bag of oranges. She walked slowly, swinging her hips, then stepped round him and closed the door. He was surprised. Why had she broken her long silence? Had she come to the end of her patience? Did she need a man? His hand went up to his thick black moustache, twirling it.

'Inshallah good news, Om Sa'd?' he asked.

'Neither good nor bad, Abu Sa'd,' she replied. 'Just God's plain truth.' She turned her back on him and stared out of the window, then turned round again to face him. 'Look, Abu Sa'd. God commanded us to cover our shame and that of our neighbours. But things can get too much. It goes beyond what one can bear when someone goes around boasting . . .' Her voice quivered with indignation and suppressed tears.

'What on earth are you talking about?'

She struck her bosom with the flat of her hand.

'I'm your wife in the eyes of God and his Prophet. I've been a good wife to you and I'm bringing up your son, may God preserve him from evil. Now I don't want to harm anybody, but if you go and marry a young slut who boasts to me of what you do with her –'

110

A smile broke over his bewildered features. So that was it.

'Come on, Om Sa'd. She's only a young girl. I had hoped she would be of use to you and serve you –'

'She's no business showing me the marks you make on her.'

'What marks?'

'Oh yes. You pretend you don't know? She showed me the big blue bite on her right buttock. "See how my man marks me," she says, wiggling her bum at me –'

'Blue what? Shut up, woman, *shut up*.' The oranges scattered on Zeina's bed as he rushed from the room.

He burst into Tahiyya's room and slammed the door behind him.

'Pull up your shift.'

The girl stood in the middle of the room.

'What?'

She had known him to be urgent. But like this? And he looked as though he were angry, with a red face and –

'Pull up your shift, woman,' he yelled.

She pulled up her shift.

'The neighbours'll hear you,' she muttered uncertainly, standing in the middle of the room.

'Come over here.' With one hand he grabbed her arm, with the other he jerked down her pants and stood staring at the big blue mark on her right buttock. She gasped as the blow landed.

'Where did you get this? Who did it?' he thundered.

'Did what?' she gasped, trying to break free.

'This, you whore, *this*.' His hand was in her hair,

tugging her head back over her shoulder to look at herself. 'This bite.'

'What bite?' she wailed. 'I don't know. I swear I don't know –'

'You don't know? Maybe this will remind you,' reaching down for his slipper. She screamed. The way he twisted her neck was breaking her spine and the sharp blows of the leather slipper rained over her body, her face, her head.

'I swear by my father's death, by the life of the Prophet, I don't know –'

'Then I'll tell you. *I'll* tell you. You bitch. You whore. You got it from "your man", your lover. Who is he? Tell me so that I can find him and drink his blood. I swear if you weren't Sheikh Mahgoub's daughter, I'd murder you this instant. Get your clothes together and get off to your mother's, you bitch. You're divorced. You're divorced three times over and I don't want ever to see your face again. I've a mind to drag you out into the street and make a spectacle of you, you dirty slut –'

Curious neighbours were gathering at their windows and on rooftops. Zeina took her time, lining her eyes with kohl and rubbing scent between her breasts. She walked out of her room, slowly, hips swaying, and into the other room:

'Stop it, Abu Sa'd, stop. Stop it, man, you'll do yourself an injury. She's not worth it. Get your clothes together, girl, and get out.'

'You don't know what she's done,' he cried, distracted. 'You don't know what the bitch has done –'

'Whatever she did, it's done, and there's no undoing

it. It's generous to forgive. Come now, come. Let her alone now. You've divorced her thrice, haven't you? She deserved it. Don't do this to yourself –'

She led him out and into her room and closed the door. He was shaking as she laid him down on the bed and bent over him tenderly:

'Lie down and rest now. The water's hot for your bath and you'll have a dinner of okra that you'll devour your own fingers after . . .'

The Apprentice

It is late spring. The sea lies smooth and quiet. The Cataract Gardens are settling into the evening, and gracious buildings in old yellow stone glow quietly in the fading light. Two of these buildings stand close together, divided by a narrow, but treed, alley. The side of one of them is blind, and on it hangs a huge billboard. It carries a crude drawing of a giant bed with a bare mattress. On the mattress a woman lies in a classic 'sexy' pose: prone, both legs bent at the knee and raised, ankles crossed. She rests on her elbows and smiles into the black telephone receiver she holds with one hand. A disconnected wire dangles from the receiver. Her other hand toys idly with a strand of yellow hair. She wears a striped green and white dress with a deep décolletage and high-heeled green open shoes with ankle straps. The legend over her head reads, 'I *always* prefer Dunlop.'

Down in the alley, by a shallow, spreading puddle, stands a boy. He is small and dark. He is dressed in faded striped green pyjama trousers and a torn brown nylon tee-shirt. He wears brown plastic sandals and he is gazing up at the vision on the billboard, his mouth half open in a dazed smile. He never even hears the horn, and the orange and black taxi has to swerve as it swings into the alley, spattering him with mud. The driver leans out of the window: 'Wake up, you donkey son of a dog. Can't you hear the horn?'

The boy turns away from the Dunlop lady and gazes after the taxi. Then he starts to walk. He walks up the narrow alley and when he comes to the main street he turns right. He makes his way west, away from the mellow, fashionable part of Alexandria, towards the harbour area where the crooked houses huddle together and the streets smell of fish and dust.

In a large, light, sparkling kitchen a stout woman in a peasant smock stands by the sink drying the silverware. As she finishes each knife, fork or spoon she lays it down carefully in a compartmented, green-baize-lined drawer. When she has put away the last one, she closes the drawer and spreads the tea-towel out to dry on the towel rack. Then she walks over to the kitchen door and takes down the long, loose, black dress hanging behind it. She pulls it on over her head and smooths it down over the flowered smock. She bends down and reaches under the fridge for her slippers. Holding them in one hand, she takes down her black *tarha* and wraps it round her head. Then she tucks her slippers under her arm and pads on thick brown feet out into the corridor. She turns left, then left again into a shaded, chintzy sitting-room with french windows open on to a wide balcony overlooking the sea. Toys of a hundred bright colours lie scattered on the white rug, and deep in a turquoise armchair a young woman nurses a small child. Her embroidered white dressing-gown is open and the baby's small black head nestles cosily against her breast. Her slippered feet rest on the seat of a small chair. 'Is there anything else you want, Set Nadia?'

The young woman looks up, smiling.

'Have you finished, Om Yosri?'

'Yes.'

'All right. Thank you. No, I don't think there's anything else. You'll bring the white aubergines with you in the morning?'

'God willing.'

'Good.'

She looks down at her baby.

'How's your back today?'

'It's better, thanks be to God. I still get a twinge now and then but, thanks be to God, it's better.'

'You must carry on with the treatment, you know.'

'Yes, of course. I know.'

Om Yosri nods vigorously.

'All right, then. Go in safety.'

'God keep you safe.'

Half-way down the corridor, she hears her name called.

'Yes? Yes, Set Nadia?'

Hurrying back.

'I say, Om Yosri, has your boy found work yet?'

'Who? Yosri? No. No, not yet.'

She makes a helpless gesture with her free hand and folds it with the other across her stomach as she launches into a favourite grievance.

'I don't know what to do with him. I apprenticed him

to an electrician, but he lasted only three days. They said they had no use for him. And the same in the car repair shop. His mind isn't on it. But he's not stupid. He never had any trouble at school –'

'You should have let him stay on. He would have learnt something –'

'What would he have learnt, Set Nadia? How to be a gentleman? Don't take it badly, but gentlemen can't make enough to eat these days. I want him to learn a trade.'

'How old is he now?'

'Fourteen, may I live to see your son his age.'

'Oh. I thought he was younger. When he came here the other day, I thought he looked quite delicate.'

'God bless you, Set Nadia. He told me how you made him come in and eat. "She's such a kind, beautiful lady, Mother," he said to me. "The most beautiful lady I've ever seen" –'

'Well, look, Om Yosri. Monsieur Hassan, my hairdresser, is looking for a boy to work in the salon. He'll start by cleaning the shop and running errands, but he'll get good tips and he'll learn a trade. And hairdressers make gold, you know. What do you say?

'Why not? I've tried him at men's jobs and he can't get on. Maybe he'll get on at the hairdresser's.'

'Right, then. We're agreed. Bring him with you tomorrow morning and I'll take him with me to the salon.'

'God preserve your children for you, Set Nadia. We're loaded with your favours –'

The Apprentice

'And, Om Osri, *don't* let him wear those striped pyjamas. Hasn't he got a pair of trousers?'

'No, I swear, Set Nadia. You know how it is: his eldest brother steals everything he can lay his hands on. He'd steal the kohl from my eyes if –'

'All right, all right. I'll see what I can do. Just bring him with you in the morning.'

Om Yosri closed the door softly behind her and slowly climbed down the stairs. She came out of the building and turned right, then right again into the treed alley. She did not notice the smiling Dunlop lady but walked heavily westward towards the harbour.

On a warm morning in early summer, a young boy stands outside the heavy, smoked-glass doors of the Salon Romance. He is dressed in blue jeans, a light blue cotton tee-shirt and a pair of brown leather sandals. He is hanging out large, soft, lilac towels with purple edging. He lays them out carefully on the mobile clothes-horse, stretching and caressing away every crease. He looks up at the bright sun: they should be dry in no time. Then he opens the dark door and steps back inside.

The salon stands at the entrance of a small cul-de-sac on one of the gentle hills of downtown Alexandria. Standing in front of it you can – if you crane a little – see the Mediterranean. The other end of the street, the dead one, has been annexed by the car repair shop, and various machines stand around with yawning bonnets while men and boys in greasy overalls attend to them with burners, paint and polish. There is a government

Co-op and there is also the coffee shop which services both the salon and the garage.

The boy must have noticed all this when he first came here. But now it is as if he no longer sees it, so engrossed is he in his work in the Salon Romance.

As he enters the salon, he has to stand for a moment blinking. Then his eyes adjust to the dim light and he threads his way through the hum of voices and the clink of instruments and round the curving white dressing-tables to the back of the room. He pushes aside the purple and gold bead curtain and goes into the 'office'. He takes a brass tray from where it stands in a corner and goes out into the salon. He wanders around, quietly collecting used coffee cups and tea glasses. In the street, he transfers them to a battered tin tray and leaves them outside the door to be picked up by the boy from the coffee shop. Then he makes another round. Crystal ashtrays overflow with slim, lipstick-stained, gold-banded stubs. For the hundredth time he marvels at the invention of the Creator: even their cigarette stubs are different.

Monsieur Hassan, moving towards the cash desk with a departing customer, looked around. It was a good day. But then, *all* days were good at the Salon Romance. He had been right to splash out on the décor. That was what the ladies wanted, and whatever the ladies wanted, he made sure they got. And what they wanted most of all was a change. A little holiday in a different, dramatic, make-believe world. Ah, Monsieur Hassan understood them so well.

'A canopy?' his wife had repeated. 'A lilac canopy draped over the ceiling? Why?'

'Just make it,' he had snapped. 'I'm not asking you to understand it. Just to make it.'

'Two S-shaped dressing-tables in the middle of the floor? Whatever for?' his friends had asked. 'What's wrong with the old side-by-side arrangement along the wall?'

'This is different,' he had said. 'And more –' he searched for a word – 'more intimate.'

Purple, velour-covered armchairs under the hair-dryers, purple and gold Italian ceramic floor-tiles; rose-tinted mirrors. And the lighting: lighting was so important; the dark, heavy glass of the shop-front tamed the sun's rays and protected the privacy of the salon. Trained spotlights illuminated crucial working areas but left many discreet shadows where the ladies could whisper, rest, or dream. And it had worked. Look at them now: the four seats at the dressing-tables were full, and so were two of the dryers; Madame Nadia was having her hair washed, Madame Aisha and Mademoiselle Mimi, in Alexandria for the summer, were sitting with old Madame Angèle waiting to be done. And the staff: all of them busy. He would soon have to get a second manicurist. Also the new boy was doing well. Madame Nadia had made him a gift there. The boy was good-looking. And quiet. Too quiet? Well, the ladies like him. And he's smart and works hard: collecting ashtrays, cups, glasses, wiping surfaces, sweeping hair off the floor, handing out rollers. Maybe he'll liven up when he gets used to things. He still goes round looking dazed, like now, taking Mademoiselle Mimi's coffee cup – 'No, no. Leave it, Yosri. Madame Angèle is going to tell my fortune. Aren't you, Madame?'

Madame Angèle raised her thin, pencilled eyebrows, '*Chérie*, did I not tell you I prefer the tarot?'

'But, Madame, you promised,' said Mimi, pouting. 'Last time you were at our place you promised –'

'I was ready to read your cards then. But didn't you whisper, "Not in front of Mama?" What would poor Safi have done to you?'

'Madame Angèle, please, *please* read the cup.'

The old lady turned to Aisha and sighed. She turned back to the small china cup and put out her right hand: pick it up, swirl it round, turn it over . . .

Yosri opened the door of the salon and put another tray on the pavement outside. The cup rims were stained with a variety of different-coloured lipsticks: pink and red and plum and – he went back inside. From the 'office' he picked up his brush and pan, then he went to the dressing-tables to collect the ladies' discarded hair; shiny black crescents where Mademoiselle Paulette had had her monthly trim, long chestnut locks under the chair where Madame Nadia had finally decided on a rebellious '*coup de garçon*' and where she was now enjoying a '*massage révitalisant*'. As he crouched, sweeping, he saw her stretch a bare foot. 'This is the best bit in the whole procedure,' she murmured. Pierre, the Coptic stylist standing behind her, smiled. '*Merci, Madame.*' He settled his fingertips more firmly on to her wet scalp and rubbed. 'A little friction is always good for the circulation,' he said in a low, confiding voice. Nadia did not answer. But she smiled and held her head upright and watched him steadily in the mirror. Now his hands were cupping her head; four fingertips behind each ear, thumbs at the crown, pressing hard, and rubbing slowly, in circles. Slowly she closed her eyes. He shifted his fingers to the back of her neck.

How pretty she was. Just a few weeks ago, Yosri had thought she was the prettiest lady in the world, and now his world was full of Set Nadias. No. *Madame* Nadias. And they were all different; some were tall and slender and long-legged, some were small, some were plump and soft and rounded, some were white as cream and some were the colour of the toffee his mother had once brought home from a birthday in the big house. Some had long hair and some had short and oh, the different ways they wore it, and the different colours. And their nails were coloured too. He had never seen feet with painted toenails before. He *had* seen plenty of women's feet, of course. But they'd been different. Madame Nadia's looked so delicate, stretched out on the rail under the dressing-table, arched and tipped with red. If he just put out his hand –

'Monsieur Hassan,' cried a lady, struggling free of a giant hairdryer, 'Monsieur Hassan, did they not get any chicken at the Co-op this week? Did you forget I asked you to buy me three pairs?'

'Monsieur Hassan does not care for us any more,' complained Madame Aisha. 'I've been begging him to put in a word for me at the mechanic's up the road and he's done nothing.'

'Oh, but I *have*, Madam Aisha,' Monsieur Hassan

cried. 'I *have*. And he says you are welcome to bring your car in. He and his men are at your service. And at the service of all our clients. Shall I book an appointment for you for next week?'

'What a good idea,' exclaimed Mimi. 'The cars can be serviced while we have our hair done.'

'It looks as if he's going to get a lot of customers.'

'You should charge him a commission, Monsieur Hassan.'

Yosri took the dustpanful of lifeless hair behind the beaded curtain. He lifted the lid off the large grey bin and slowly poured in the hair. Poor, dusty locks. So glorious as they tumbled through Monsieur Hassan's and the other men's fingers, so dull when they came to the bin. He put the lid back and went out to collect the damp towels from around the basins.

For weeks now he has watched the ladies settle soft hips into soft leather, poise their heads delicately on the sloping head-rests and stream their hair into the lilac basins. Braceleted wrists and jewelled fingers dangle from the arm-rests, surrendered. He has watched the slim, tight-trousered juniors brace themselves behind the basins, feet apart. They hold each head with infinite, yet unworried care; precious eggshells, fragile, yet familiar to their expert hands. They rub and stroke and pull and brush and the ladies lie back with closed eyes and gleaming lips. He has heard them complain when the hand-shower is held over their hair: 'Oh, oh, that's *far* too hot. Are you trying to burn me?' Or, 'Darling, that's *desperately* cold. You'll give me pneumonia.' And sometimes, clasping lilac towels to their necks with bright-nailed fingers, 'Oooh, the water's running down my back – oh *do* take care.' And always the quiet, respectful response. 'Of course, Madame.'

'What's all this? What's all this?' Madame Gabi had walked through the door. 'May God increase and bless it. Every seat taken? Well, Monsieur Hassan, you'll have to start a café on the *trottoir* outside for customers who have to wait. Or would that distract the mechanics next door? Here, Yosri, take my jacket and hang it up. From the loop, mind, not the collar. Or do you have a proper hanger you can put it on? Yes, all right, take it into the office – oh no, no, wait. Heaven knows *what* you keep in there. Leave it out here. I'll put it on the back of Monsieur Hassan's chair. *That's* right. Now run and fetch me some boiling water from the coffee shop. Just a glassful of *boiling water*, mind. Don't let them put anything in it. I've got my own tea-bags right here. Run along. Quickly. What a pretty boy he's turning into. Monsieur Hassan, have you been curling his hair?'

'No, no, I assure you. It's natural. We just use the salon shampoo and conditioner and it dries like that.'

'And that lovely, toasted colour and those sad eyes. He should wear a chain. A gold chain round his neck. He'd look a sugar with a gold chain –'

'He should wear an ear-ring. Men abroad wear ear-rings now, you know. Not a pair, just one.' That was Aisha.

'Oh, those are the you-know-whats. No *real* man would ever wear an ear-ring –'

'Oh yes they do. It's the fashion. And anyway, pirates used to wear them.'

127

'So who says pirates weren't poofs? They used to spend months without women –'

'Ah, but look what they did with the women once they found them.'

'Maybe they worked both ways. Took what they could find. Sometimes a boy, sometimes a woman –'

'Sometimes a fish.' The Salon Romance rang with laughter.

'But what do *you* think, Monsieur Hassan? Shouldn't he wear jewellery?'

'Not an ear-ring, no,' said Monsieur Hassan, smiling. 'But perhaps the chain is a good idea. It would be an ideal way for him to save his money anyway. An investment.'

'He can save up his tips.'

'He'd have to. He turns all his wages over to his mother.'

'Great. Let's have a fund. You put a box on the cash-desk, Monsieur Hassan. Then any lady who wants to tip him can put the money in it. And when there's enough money, we'll buy him a gold chain with a pendant. He'll be the envy of every apprentice on the street.'

It is a stifling September day. Yosri is gathering the towels from the clothes-horse. He has grown taller and wears tight white denims and a dark blue shirt. The shirt is unbuttoned half-way and on his chest a gold chain with a Pisces pendant catches the sun. He is quicker now, less hesitant in his movements. Mimi's green Fiat draws up and he steps forward, smiling, to help her out.

'Your boy has learned quickly,' she comments to

Monsieur Hassan, as she watches Yosri carry the pile of neatly folded towels into the office.

'Yes, he's a good boy. I let him lock up shop now after we've all gone. And he's the first one here in the morning. He's bright. He's been practising washing the assistants' hair and they think he's getting quite good.'

'You must let him try a client soon.'

'Yes, I know. But we'll have to wait until someone brings in a child, or we get some passing trade or something. I can't let him try on one of my regulars.'

'Why not? *I'm* willing to try him. If he's no good I'll just call for someone else.'

Yosri stood by the basin, holding a towel. His day had come. He was going to do it; he was going to touch one of them. Mademoiselle Mimi with the light brown hair, the wide hips and the slim ankles. He watched her settle into the chair, then he bent and draped the towel carefully round her shoulders, and she, smiling, put up her hands and tucked it into the neck of her turquoise shirt. With both hands he lifted the long hair from her nape and she laid her head back against the head-rest and closed her eyes.

He planted his feet firmly apart and turned on the hand-shower. He tested the water on his hand, adjusting the temperature till it was pleasantly cool but with no edge of coldness. He let it play on his hand till he was sure it was constant, then he started gently watering Mimi's hair. He held the hand-shower over the top of her brow, cupping it so that the water would not stream over her face. Then he moved it to the back of her head. He parted the dampened hair and gently pushed the shower into it, making sure it got soaked through. He put the shower down in the basin and poured some cold shampoo into his hand. He kept it there for a moment to warm it, then he lightly rubbed his hands together and passed them over the hair. Then he started to rub: he rubbed the scalp, he lifted strands of hair and rubbed them carefully against each other and let them fall.

He took up his hand-shower and rinsed. Again the shampoo. This time he worked it into a full and foamy lather. And now his fingers slid easily in and out of the slippery hair; he massaged the top of the head, and the back, and both sides, then the back again. He watched his fingers emerge from the soapy hair at both sides of Mimi's head and reach towards the ears; two slim middle fingers found the small earholes and poked curiously, delicately, in. He pressed himself against the back of the basin. The skin behind her ears was so fine and smooth and stretched so taut over the fragile bone. He pressed, and his fingers slid into the little soft hollow just behind each lobe. 'Shall I leave the cream on the hair a couple of minutes, Mademoiselle?' he asked, bending over her.

'Yes,' Mimi whispered without opening her eyes.

He swept the hair up and settled it in one shining mass on top of her head. Slowly and tenderly he dried her forehead and temples with a piece of cotton wool. Then he went into the office.

He leaned against the wall, his hands pushing deep into his pockets. He had never felt this before; every drop of his blood racing towards one focal point, leaving his legs weak and his mind hazy. How was he going to get through the day? Would they all notice? It was wonderful. More wonderful than anything he'd ever dreamed or read about. But he had to go. He had to go. She was waiting for him. He levered himself away from the wall, pulled his hands from his pockets and took up his position behind the basin.

Later, holding the lilac towel to her neck, Mimi addressed Monsieur Hassan in the styling mirror: 'The boy is a born *coiffeur*; he has a real feeling for hair.'

Monsieur Hassan, deftly smoothing wet hair on to large, pink rollers, smiled. 'Thanks be to God. His heart's in the job.'

'Yosri,' called the manicure girl, 'fill a pedicure basin for Madame Gabi.'

Yosri filled a purple plastic tub with tepid water, added a squirt of detergent and a drop of jasmine essence. He carried it carefully into the salon and put it at Madame Gabi's feet as she sat under the dryer. She shook off her shoes and slipped her feet into the water. Then she pushed the dryer off her head.

'So you were telling me – he asked her to go home with him?' Madame Gabi turned to the plump blonde sitting beside her, hands spread on her knees waiting for her nails to dry.

'Oh yes,' she said, nodding, 'and he openly said he had some naughty films he could show her.'

'Hah? And?'

'Well, you know Zizi. She looks so *douce* and *bien élevée*. But she's really tough underneath and she said, "Go home with *you*? Not likely. I know all about you and how *tu aimes frapper les femmes*."'

'Heavens! What did *he* say?'

'Nothing. His face went white and he turned round and walked out. He's not been to the office since.'

'Poor man. *Non, vraiment.* I pity him. After all, a lot of men are like that. And, *entre nous*, it's not *that* bad –'

'No, no, my dear. You don't understand.' The blonde, fingers still carefully spread out, leaned forward and placed a hand on her friend's knee. 'There is a difference. A lot of men . . . *avant, oui, peut-être. Mais après? Jamais. C'est de la perversion, alors?*'

The last customer, coiffed and happy, had departed. Monsieur Hassan and his assistants had washed their faces, combed their hair, and left in a jangle of car and motorcycle keys. Yosri was alone in the Salon Romance with the final job of locking up. He looked around him: crystal ashtrays overflowed with lipstick-stained cigarette ends, locks of hair gathered dust on the tiled floor, damp towels lay draped over the arms of chairs, pink rollers frothed blowsily out of their wicker baskets and an empty shampoo bottle oozed its last golden viscous drops into the lilac basin. It would take at least an hour to clear up. He felt strange. The immediate urge which had possessed him so strongly in the afternoon had passed and now he was tired and reflective. The day which had been so hot and heavy had turned, no doubt, into a benign and breezy evening. He would clear up the salon early tomorrow morning and tonight he would just walk slowly home. He would walk along the corniche. He had some money in his pocket, for now that the chain had been bought, the ladies were giving him his tips in cash – till they thought up some other scheme.

He could stop along the way and have a sandwich and a glass of sugar cane juice. And he could think about what had happened.

He moved around the salon, switching off the spotlights. In the dark, he collected the keys and made for the door. As he reached it, it opened and the doorway was filled by a large figure. Yosri could not see clearly, for what light there was came from the dim street-lamp outside and the stranger was blocking most of it. Yosri could only see him in silhouette. Then he made out the overalls and heavy shoes and knew it was one of the mechanics from the garage up the street. But which one? Did he know him? He knew none of them, really. And why had he come here? The man stepped aside and let the heavy door swing shut. It locked into place as he leant back against it. Why did he not speak? A sudden heavy weight formed in the boy's stomach and he felt his legs go weak and warm. His palms were sweating and he dug his hands into his pockets. The man took one slow step forward and reached out. His hand brushed against the boy's chest as he carefully took hold of the chain and began stroking the golden fish with his thumb.

The Nativity

*T*heir steps rang out on the cobbles of the old square. It was late May and raining. Aisha found the rain pleasant. The drops were small and sharp and fast and slanted. The air was crisp and the moon was out in the black sky and the cobbles gleamed and she was happy. She lifted her face to the sky and let her hair get wet. I watched her husband draw close and again offer her his umbrella. But she did not want its protection. She wanted nothing to come between her and the rain and the sky. So he walked on. Dry.

It had been her idea that they should park in the road below and climb the two hundred steps up to the top of the hill. He had not wanted to. It was impractical, he had said. They were in evening dress, they could be mugged. The car, left on a dark street, could be broken into. What was the point? Normally she would have anticipated all this. She would have suppressed her impulse. Tonight, she had stepped outside habit. She had pressed him. 'It will be so nice later,' she had coaxed. 'When the party's over, it'll be lovely to walk down all these steps – and there will be a full moon.' He had given in and parked.

Now the old, white cathedral rose silent above them.

They walked into its shadow and emerged into the moonlight on the other side. In front of them, like a fantasy set in an extravagant production, the broad marble steps shimmered down towards the narrow street and the unseen, waiting car.

As they emerged from the darkness of the cathedral, a third figure joined them. It hung behind a little, a fragment of black shadow, then slipped around to Aisha's side. It laid a thin, brown hand on her arm. 'Ten francs,' it whispered. 'For just ten francs, Madame, I tell your fortune.' Aisha looked down. Dark eyes met dark eyes, but the stranger hooded hers instantly. Aisha stopped. The hand was lifted from her arm and slowly revolved to remain outstretched, palm upwards. 'No. No, thank you —' Aisha began, conscious of her husband, waiting, separate under his umbrella. 'Give me your hand. The right,' a changed voice said. Aisha held out her right hand and placed it, palm upwards, in the still outstretched hand that waited for it. The stranger let it lie. She did not bother with the formality of tracing the lines with her forefinger. Why should she? She did not even look down at the white palm she held in her own. She kept her hooded eyes on Aisha. Beautiful Aisha giving off light in the dark before us.

'You carry darkness, my child. In season, with the year. In its beginning its end will be. Too close. You should not have gone so close.'

Aisha was standing, listening. The stranger faded back into a shadow and disappeared. But Aisha's hand was still stretched out, palm upwards, open to the rain. Her husband moved to her side and took her arm to draw her under his umbrella. 'Come,' he said, 'you'll catch your death of cold.' In his hand he held the ten franc note the stranger had forgotten to take. It was only then – almost three months too late – that I knew.

Early in March

I had watched them carefully over the years. Sometimes they argued. But less and less as time went by. Aisha learnt to be careful. To avoid certain subjects. To avoid enthusiasms, excesses, tears. To avoid – me. It was not that she was afraid of him. I believe she was afraid *for* him; afraid of me. And she wanted to go on loving him.

Once, in a restaurant, talking about a long-dead Eastern mystic, she burst into angry, helpless tears:

'Why should you think you know *everything*? O.K., so you believe in science. Why can't you think that maybe what sounds like nonsense today has a scientific explanation that will be discovered tomorrow?'

'Nonsense,' he said, smiling. 'There isn't a scientific explanation for the "Third Eye".'

'How do you know? And how do you know there *won't* be?'

'There won't,' he said, and shrugged.

'So you believe that everything there is to be known has *been* known. Like everything there is to do has *been* done. There won't ever be anything new? *Ever again*? So why don't we just *die*? Why don't we die? *Now*?'

139

She was crying, and everyone wondered at the passion that overtook and shook and made her weep in the elegant restaurant, surrounded by the husband and family who loved her so much. After all, what was another Eastern mystic to her, or she to him, that she should display such passion in his defence?

My poor and precious darling. I hated to feel happy while she was in such despair. But it was only in despair that she was with me; not pushing me out of her life, denying me. It was not my fault that my presence caused her such unhappiness. It did not have to be so.

I knew that she was aware of me. Even if, most of the time, she found it expedient to pretend I did not exist. But I would not let her rest. I would lie low for days, lurking in dark corners until she came upon me. I would feel her recognise me. And then she should fight. But she knew. I know she knew.

So when her old nurse whispered in her ear that maybe someone had laid a curse on her so that she would not conceive, she listened.

'Is it not possible?' asked the old woman. 'Who knows? You are young and beautiful and fortunate and you draw the Evil Eye.'

'Who on earth is going to curse me, Dada?' asked Aisha. 'And why in this particular thing?'

'There is a knot that must be broken,' said her nurse, looking up at her with one good eye.

There is a knot but it will not be broken. How can it be broken when she does not love him? Does not love him as a woman should love her man. When even as he enters her, she is closed to him. When even as he probes her, she retreats from him. For I have seen them in their soft and delicate bedroom amid laced and ruffled pillowcases. And I have seen her turn away from the vague pleasantness of his face when he tentatively sought to arouse her passion, and shrink from the rigid mask of his features when he surrendered unwillingly to his own. I have seen her turn her head away and drift among the whirling cornices of the walls or the intricate lace of her pillow. And I have seen them, when by accident their glances met, swiftly exchange the polite apologetic smiles of strangers stubbing each other's toes on a crowded bus.

'You have done everything the doctors asked, poor child. Everything. Haven't you? They've poked and prodded and burnt and painted. Is that not the truth?'

'I know.'

'And the master. He's gone along with it too. He's let them look at him, handle him, squeeze him. He can't have liked it, you know. Men don't like that sort of thing. Do you want him to doubt himself? That's no good for a man. *You* must do something.'

Aisha listened to her nurse as she had been listening to her for twenty-seven years. Oh, Zeina, Zeina. You think yourself so wise. You believe you know all about her: your first nurseling, your pride, the apple of your eye, slipping silently in through the back door, her fingers on her lips. 'Hush! Don't tell, don't tell.' Pulling off her high and secret heels for you to hide before wandering innocently off to greet her parents. Her parents. Much more your child than theirs. Did you know that all along? The time is right, now, and you will remind her of us; of me. And she will listen as she used to, long ago.

'All right. So let's say no one's laid a curse on you. Maybe you've done something. Maybe you've made them angry —'

'"Them?" Who's "them?" We're going back to talk of "them" now, Dada? We left all that behind long ago.'

'Hush, child. Don't talk like that. They hear you, God forgive us. They're our familiars, my darling, our masters. And we have to please and satisfy them or they clamp on our heads and never let us rest. You know all this. I've told you a thousand stories since you were tiny. And you used to listen and ask for more.'

Wise woman. Wise old woman. The smell of frying coriander rising sweet and sharp from your wooden spoon as your child goes to and fro between your kitchen and their dining-room. Tell her now. Tell her about Sidi Abul Suoud, the Saint, and his wife, Set Habiba. Aisha has always loved your stories.

'I won't say you should go to some far-off shrine. And I won't say set up a *zar* of your own. But what's the harm in going to visit Sidi Abul Suoud, the Saint? I'll come with you. We'll go and visit him and pray for him. And we'll pray for his wife and ask her to put in a word for you. Tell her how much you need a child.'

'And what does all this have to do with "them"?'

'They have Presences there every Tuesday. We'll go and see. Maybe your knot will be broken. God is generous, my child.'

Yes. God is generous, and his generosity can manifest itself in many forms.

142

The Nativity

Tuesday

The sandy hill on the border of the city and the Eastern Desert is overrun. There are donkey-carts loaded with bright orange mandarins. There are barrows full of cheap sweets, paper caps, whistles, little clay piggy-banks and drums of many sizes, tinsel jewellery, and tasselled prayer-beads. A man sits cross-legged on a cart, fanning the sweet corn grilling over charcoal. He is surrounded by little hills of corn cobs still nestling inside their pale green husks. Occasionally he selects one, tears it out of its protective leaves and places it carefully on the burning coal. When it is ready and golden, he hands it to a waiting customer.

His customers are all over the hillside; black-clad women and their children. They are everywhere. Some of the women sit in small groups, talking. They eat mandarins, spit out the pips and nurse their babies. Some younger ones crowd round the jewellery stalls, bargaining over glass necklaces. Some stretch out on the dusty sand amid the mandarin peel and the green discarded corn leaves and, pulling their tarhas over their faces for protection against the dust and the myriad flies, they fall asleep. No men are there except the ones with business; the ones with something to sell.

The gathering on the hill is flanked by the wide highway that embraces the eastern side of Cairo, separating the city from the Mokattam mountain and the Eastern Desert beyond; separating too, the city of the living from the City of the Dead. On the south slope there are four red, white and blue tents from which there rises the rhythmic thud of drumming. Each one has a folded-back flap for a doorway and around each doorway there is a crowd of sitting, kneeling, standing women. The hill rises from the quarter of Masr Atiqa with its ancient Christian cemeteries, and on its eastern summit sits the green-domed mosque of Sidi Abul Suoud, the Healer of Hearts.

And here they come now: two figures climbing the gradual slope of the hill and moving in among the crowd. Zeina blends in easily with her black *galabiya* and *tarha*. Aisha has obviously dressed down. She wears a pair of beige trousers she has had for seven years, some gym shoes and a creased jacket buttoned over a white cotton shirt with a worn collar. She has pulled her black hair back into a pony-tail and she wears no make-up, no jewellery, no watch. Even the gold chain with the head of Aries has vanished from round her neck and the wedding band from her finger. Even so, the women pause and follow her with their eyes. I am proud of her, and happy, and yes – I am expectant. I am hoping that today she will give me some sign; say some word that she will not be able later to recant or disown.

'What is she? What brings her?'

'Is she a foreigner, or what?'

'No, no, she looks native.'

'Maybe she's a journalist?'

'We don't want any journalists here –'

Suddenly the mosque seems too far away to the old woman and she starts manoeuvring her charge to the right and towards the shelter of the nearest tent.

'We'll visit the Saint later,' she says. 'Let's go into a Presence first.'

They push through the crowd at the doorway, the nurse tapping the backs of the women with one hand, 'With your permission, sister, with your permission,' and drawing Aisha behind her with the other. Aisha pays the entrance fee to the girl at the door and they shoulder their way in. They step carefully over the women and children crammed on the floor and make for the farthest corner. The old woman sits herself down on the floor, but Aisha remains standing; she leans against the corner and folds her arms.

The air is full of smoke and the perfume of fresh sweat mixing with the smell of musk and amber and holy incense. There is another sweet and rather acrid smell that Aisha cannot identify.

The musicians sit at one end of the tent: four men and a woman. Their only instruments are drums and tambourines. Right now, they are having a rest. They sit on their straw mat smoking bulky, hand-rolled joints, talking and keeping an eye on their audience. Aisha looks at their joints and realises that she is smelling the sweetness of hashish for the first time. She registers the difference between the performers and their audience: the woman musician is sitting at her ease; her left leg tucked under her, the right leg raised and bent at the knee to support the wrist of the hand holding the joint. She wears a long, flowered *galabiya* and her head is tied with a red kerchief which reveals the greater part of her long hair. Her sleeves are rolled up and her arms are solid with gold bracelets. Gold teeth reflect the glint of the bracelets and she wears rouge and green eyeshadow as well as the kohl all the women use to rim the insides of their eyes. Her broad, coarse feet are tipped with bright, chipped scarlet.

I see Aisha give a gentle, absent kick to a small hand that has inserted itself between the ground and the tapestry and is groping around her ankle.

The musicians are getting themselves ready. They pinch out their joints and store them in their pockets. They hand their empty tea glasses back to the girl at the door. Two men holding tambourines stand up and the painted woman adjusts the bosom of her *galabiya* and tucks her drum under her left arm, giving it a few taps with her fingers. The women on the floor become animated, calling out the names of various rhythms.

One of the men grins, showing a gap in the middle of large black teeth. He unwinds his turban and his hair falls long and straight to his shoulders. He has brilliant, kohled, black eyes and a tattered grey *galabiya* stopping inches above thin white feet and ankles.

As the rhythm begins to emerge, individual women detach themselves from their groups and move towards the rectangle of floor space that has been left empty in front of the musicians. Children are left behind. Babies are thrust into the arms of the nearest unmoved neighbours as the women to whose familiars this particular rhythm belongs move obediently towards the floor. First they move slowly, lifting and dropping their heels like lazy cyclists, eyes on the floor before them. Slightly embarrassed, perhaps, in front of the musicians and the watching audience. Then, as the beat gets louder and more commanding, the masters take over, claiming the bodies that are theirs. The women jump and reel. They fling and toss their heads. Their eyes are closed. The children sit quietly on the floor, gazing upon the abandon of their mothers: the *tarhas* flung off, the kerchiefs loosened, hair spilling everywhere. Upraised arms cause hems of black *galabiyas* to rise, showing smooth brown legs; some bare and adorned with thick metal anklets; some covered by the legs of flowered pyjama trousers; all stamping, twisting, whirling – oh look, look how these women dance, see how they surrender themselves to their masters, look, take it all in, and understand.

It's a Bacchanalia, Aisha thinks, eyes riveted on the blind, enraptured faces. One woman dances serenely; her long black lashes lying quiet, her brow smooth, the smallest of smiles brushing a corner of her mouth. Another knits her forehead tight in concentration, the tip of her tongue caught between her teeth and curling to touch her upper lip. Many adopt attitudes of supplication. A few gnash their teeth and pull at their hair. It's a Bacchanalia, she whispers to herself in wonderment. How strange. Yes. How strange that you should have read about it; that as a child you should have brooded over pictures in big, fat books. While I waited. All those years I waited. And then you dismissed it all. You decided it was a world that had happened long ago, long ago in far-off places. By what right did you decide? With what knowledge? And now? Will you see that it is here? That all the time it was here? On your doorstep, waiting for you?

A hand plucks at her trouser leg through the tapestry, and again she nudges it away.

One of the tambourine men singles out two women for special attention. They are less abandoned than the rest, more measured in their steps, reluctant to yield. He brings them together and puts the hands of one into the hands of the other. He beats and jangles his tambourine between their heads and shouts along with the rhythm. Soon they too are calling out, hands clasped fast together, heads swaying, *tarhas* loose around their shoulders. Now the drumming rises to its climax and one by one the whirling, sweating women begin to stumble and fall. Some grope their way towards their original places and fall in a panting heap by their children. Some dance to the very end, then pick their way shakily back, eyes lowered in the silence. One woman collapses in the middle of the floor and lies writhing and sobbing. A woman on the edge of the ring drags her into the audience and applies herself to reviving her as the clamouring requests for the next tune begin. Aisha has dropped to her knees and is cautiously edging her way towards the unconscious woman till she is right behind her. The stranger looking after her is bending down and putting her mouth to the stricken one's ear. 'God is great!' she cries. 'God is great! God is great!' She tilts her head, puts her mouth to the other ear and cries out her proclamation once again. Then she starts rubbing the heaving chest with one hand while she holds the shoulders steady with the other. 'In the name of God,' she says, 'have mercy on her. Have pity, for the sake of the Prophet. She's had enough, can't you see? Come, now, Brother, Master, leave her alone for a bit. You're too hard on her, really you are. See what you've done?' Aisha glances at the women surrounding them. Some make sucking, commiserating noises with their lips, but nobody is really listening. No, Aisha, no one finds it odd, the familiarity with which the woman addresses even a stranger's ruling spirit. And see how the heavy breathing subsides and soothing tears seep from her still-closed eyes? Watch. Watch.

Carefully, Aisha creeps back, squeezing through the seated women to squat on the floor next to her nurse. And I watch as she closes her eyes and leans back against the cloth wall.

The music now begins again and a playful punch from behind the wall makes her straighten up and open her eyes. Standing just inside the doorway is a newcomer; a man. A boy? No – I watch as she decides – a man . . . just about.

She can see that he is not a musician, for he carries no instrument and besides, he stands apart. He is not dressed in a *galabiya* but wears a pair of cheap black leather trousers tucked into black plastic boots that come half-way up his calves. These boots are now planted sturdily apart on the dusty floor. His hands are at his waist and the short-sleeved, blue tee-shirt bulges with vulgar muscle. His hair is frizzy and brown and close-cropped and he looks around the tent with a wide, anticipating smile. His eyes fall on Aisha and, for a moment, the smile is beamed on her – then a commotion rises in the doorway behind him and he steps aside. Two women are pushing their way loudly through the crowd. Between them they support a large,

inert figure in a flowered *galabiya* with a veil thrown
untidily over her face.

They stumble in, their arms round the woman,
dragging her, trying to reach some empty spot before
she slides from their grasp completely. The young man
at the door moves forward. He puts his arms round the
veiled woman and half drags, half carries her to the far
side of the tent, away from the door. He lays her on the
floor and the two women sink down beside her, thanking
him, praising his strength, fanning their faces with their
tarhas, mopping their brows and upper lips with large
man-sized handkerchiefs drawn from their bosoms and,
finally, turning to the one lying beside them, they adjust
her *galabiya* over her legs, straighten her neck and remove
the veil from her face. Aisha cranes: it is a girl. For all her
bulk she cannot be more than fifteen. She is fair, her hair
is untidy and damp with sweat and her eyes are open and
rolling backwards so that all you can see of them is the
whites. Her mouth is open and a thin line of spittle runs
down the side of her face. The young man looks down
at her. 'What a pity,' he says. 'She's young.'

'May God never show you this in someone, dear,' one
of the women mutters automatically as she bends to wipe
the girl's mouth. He shakes his head and, looking up, he
sees Aisha's face, thrust forward, attentive. He sees her
turn and kick impatiently at the red and blue tapestry
of the wall behind her. I watch as he steps over, placing
his boots carefully in the tiny spaces between the waiting
women. He stands before her and raises his voice above
the beat of the drums: 'The kids bothering you?' He
nods towards the wall. She nods . . . shrugs. He lifts the

tapestry, ducks and is out the other side. He moves fast. She hears him shouting, 'Hey! You! You faggot sons of bitches . . .' and she glances down at her nurse. The old woman's eyes are closed and she is rocking to the music. In a moment he is back. I know what she is thinking; he is not really tall. It's just the way he stands that made him look big across the crowded tent. And his clothes. Black leather! Oh, Aisha, Aisha . . . she smiles. He smiles back easily.

'This is the first time you come here?'

She nods. The drums are too loud for her to try to speak above them.

He inspects her. 'You Egyptian?'

She nods. I wait for the next question, but it does not come. What should she have said if he had asked which part of town she came from?

'Have you been on the floor yet?'

She shakes her head.

'Why not?' She does not answer.

'None of the beats pulled you? Or don't you have a master?' He grins, but she takes her time.

'I don't know,' she shouts.

Progress. Better than laughter. Or a denial. Then, 'Have you been up to see the Saint yet?'

She shakes her head.

'Well, when you've finished here, I'll take you up to visit him. You shouldn't really wander round here alone. But this is my patch – if you're with me no one can bother you. Oh, I'm not a *zar*-man,' he explains, seeing her look towards the musicians. 'Do I look like one of *them*?'

He draws himself up, grinning. 'They're low people;

thieves, criminals. No. I'm a butcher. A master butcher. Well . . . my father's the master butcher really. Across the road in the Slaughterhouse. But I'm his eldest. I work with him and when he gets too old for the job, it'll fall to me. Everyone knows that down there. I just come here every Tuesday because I like the music. And the dancing. Men aren't allowed here. But they know me. They know I'm not dirty. And I have sisters. And . . . well . . . this is my patch.' He stops. 'My name's Farag. Your servant.' He holds out his hand.

Aisha holds out hers, for all the world as though she were at some dinner-party: 'I'm Aisha,' she says. And they shake hands.

'I'll see you later, Aisha. But you should dance before you go. You *must* have a master. He'll pick his own beat.' Two steps away he turns back: 'Those kids won't bother you again.'

Well, well, Aisha. Attending a *zar*. Squatting in the dust. Making friends with a butcher – a *master* butcher. Oh dear, oh dear. What will your husband say? What will *everybody* say? She smiles: her aunt was emphatic. 'Don't do it, Aisha. For my sake, please don't go. You know your Uncle Rashad's daughter? Well *she* used to go off to things like that. Attending low-class *zars* and Presences. Dancing with those people. Going into a trance. Falling on the ground and rolling in the dust. Till one day she came *out* of her trance to find herself married. Those *zar*-people are wicked. They're criminal. Honestly, they'd married her to a dwarf. You would throw up if you saw him. A tiny man with a great big ugly head. And there he was, leering at her and there was her signature on the marriage certificate. Your Uncle Rashad had to come up with a thousand pounds to buy her a divorce . . .'

Aisha smiles again.

I have not seen her smile like this for a long, long time.

One beat has stopped and now another starts. It is the beat of the master of one of the two women who came in carrying the girl in the coma. Zeina is leaning against the wall, her eyes closed. Recovering from the rhythm, waiting while her master, satisfied, slips from her and leaves her peaceful. And now I watch Aisha make her way quietly on her hands and knees towards the unconscious girl. She eases herself into a space on the floor beside her and puts out a hand to touch her forehead. It is damp and cold, the eyes rolled back, the jaw slack, the mouth open. She turns to the woman with her: 'How long has she been like this?' she asks. The woman looks up, suspicious, but when Aisha gravely meets her eye, keeping her fingers on the girl's forehead, she gives in. 'Four months,' she says. 'Four months we've been spooning food into her mouth. Changing and wiping her like a baby, and she's a grown woman. God grant her mother patience. It's hard. Very hard.'

'God help you all, mother. Are you her aunt?'

'Yes, but she's like a daughter to me. We all live together, you see. Not here. Oh no. We've come from Beheira. A long way away. We've been travelling for two days. But God is generous and people have been kind to us. Pray God we won't return with broken hearts. They said her recovery would be at the hands of Sidi

Abul Suoud, the Healer of Hearts. Pray God they're right . . .'

'Have you visited?'

'Oh yes. It was the first thing we did. We prayed for him and his Lady and we carried the girl round his holy resting place seven times. Her father has sworn he'll slaughter a sheep for the poor if we come back with her cured – and he's not well off, God help him. Pray for us, child . . .'

Aisha looks down at the bulky figure. 'What brought it on?' The woman retreats into suspicion. Aisha waits. She knows the woman will speak. She is learning. The woman turns back to her. 'She saw a man murdered. She stayed out late in the field one night and on her way back she stumbled over something heavy, and when she bent down to look, it was a corpse. He was still warm, poor man, and she came home with her *galabiya* covered in blood. She's been like this since . . .'

'She's not seen a doctor?' That was the wrong thing to say.

'A doctor? What would a doctor do? This isn't a matter for doctors.'

And now Aisha edges her way back to her nurse. Zeina is looking with narrowed eyes across the room. 'What is that man doing here? He's not a *zar*-man, he's a butcher. Why do they let him in?' Sharp. Sharp and quick. 'How do you know he's a butcher?' Aisha asks. She looks up.

Farag is in the centre of the dancing women. His head is thrown back, his arms raised high. His eyes are closed. The fingers of his broad hands are spread wide. And his whole body vibrates strongly. For an instant he opens

his eyes and glances around him. His face is totally alert
and he smiles.

'A butcher from the Slaughterhouse. That's slaughterhouse clothes he's wearing.'

'Why? Why particularly slaughterhouse clothes?'

'They're plastic, child, look. Plastic and leather. Don't
you know anything? So they can hose them down when
they get covered with blood. Aren't they knee-high in
slaughter all day? But what's he doing here?' The question
is rhetorical but Aisha answers:

'He said they let him stay because they know he's a
good boy. And he likes the *zar*.'

The old woman is alarmed.

'How do you know? Did you speak to him?'

'He chased the kids away. You know, the ones who
were pinching me through the wall.'

Silence.

'And he said he'd take us up to visit the Saint later.'

'And what's wrong with our legs, then, that *he* should
take us up?'

'He says it's dangerous. We shouldn't walk round on
our own. And besides, it's his patch.'

'His what? His *patch*? So he's a strongman, is he?'
Her nurse made a derisive sound with her lips. 'We'll
have nothing to do with him.'

'Why, Dada, what's the harm? He was terribly polite.
And he chased those kids away . . .'

'We'll have nothing to do with him.'

Aisha is silent. She can see why her nurse would not
like him.

It is due to his presence that this dance is palpably

155

more charged than the previous ones. 'And all shall cry Beware! Beware! His flashing eyes, his –' Well, his hair *isn't* floating, she interrupts herself – stop being so silly. It's true. She shakes her head. Aisha, you know so much more about Art than Life. Here is Life. Life surrounds you, clamours at your ears and eyes and nostrils and you crouch in your corner beside your nurse and quote poetry. Well, poetry was never written by crouching behind one's nurse and –

'Look,' her nurse nudges her, 'look. They're going to try to make that poor girl dance. God forgive us all. She's young. May God be with her.'

The two women are hauling the unconscious girl on to the dance floor. The musicians are just limbering into the new beat, but already you can hear its pattern. 'She answered the rhythm, sisters! She answered the rhythm! Your mercy, God!' one of the women cries as they prop her up in the middle of the floor. Her head is still thrown back, her feet drag uselessly on the ground and her body is a dead weight on the supporting arms of her mother and aunt. The music speeds up and the men with the tambourines move in closer to the girl. The other women stay on the edges of the floor, allowing the little group in the middle the greatest amount of space. The mother and aunt are now trying not just to hold the girl up, but to move her body in time to the music. The aunt is supporting her as Aisha has seen people supporting drunks in films: an arm round the girl's waist and the girl's arm round her shoulders. She is trying to jump but is only able to make little bobbing movements under the weight. The girl's head has been brought forward and rests on the shoulder of her mother, who holds her up from the other side. The music grows and the two women are sweating and struggling under the weight of the girl. Now they are no longer able to move her. And now she begins to slip from them to the floor. Farag the butcher, standing watching from the doorway, steps forward. Once again he puts the two older women aside. He grabs the girl by the waist and holds her up. As the musicians bang their tambourines above her head and shout in her ears, he dances and shakes her. He leaps in the air and carries her with him. He rattles her so her head shakes giddily from side to side. Her head shakes from side to side, then steadies. Still wobbly, still uncertain, but better. The helpless eyes close and in front of Aisha's concentrating gaze, the bare, plump feet right themselves and seek uncertainly for a grip on the floor. The woman musician is pounding her drum and singing a strident, ecstatic song in time to its beat. The men with the tambourines are possessed: they whirl and leap and shout. The dancing women are kerchiefless and even the braids in their hair have been undone so that each separate strand might fly loose. And in the centre of the Presence, embraced by the butcher, the fat girl's outraged demon is being appeased at last.

I live and relive this story as I wait for her to come back to me. Was there some other way it could have gone? Should I have tried to pull her, to force her then to dance for me? I felt that she would fight; that the time was not yet right. I had waited so long, I could wait some more. And then she met her butcher.

157

Aisha and her nurse pushed through the doorway and edged their way out of the tent. The air was light and clear after the incense, the sweat and the smoke inside. Scattered noises fell less densely upon their ears, and eyes had to be shaded against the glare of the white afternoon light reflected in the dusty sand. They began to climb towards the mosque at the top of the hill. Her nurse was leaning heavily upon her and Aisha found her own knees trembling. Her head felt light and spacious, as though she had been drinking, and her eyes were smarting and, she was sure, red. The children began to gather, laughing, pointing, commenting, and then, made bold by the two women's obvious weariness, they came close and started to touch Aisha: fingering her clothes, tugging at her hands –

'Have you seen Farag the butcher?'

The question worked like magic.

'Yes, yes. I know where he is. I'll go and fetch him.' A swarm of small boys raced whooping off, back towards the tents. Her nurse said nothing. Then she asked, 'What time is it?'

Aisha shrugged. 'Didn't you say I shouldn't bring my watch? It must be around four, I suppose.'

'Four? We'd better hurry. What time did you tell your husband you'd be back?'

'I didn't.'

'You didn't? What do you mean you *didn't*?' Aisha's nurse was leaning on her arms and peering up into her face.

'You *know* he went out early. I just didn't say anything before he left.'

'You're not going to tell him?'

'That I've been here? No. No, Dada. He'll only think I'm silly.'

'Silly? Who dares call you silly?'

Farag the butcher had caught up with them. 'Have the kids been bothering you? Show me which ones and I'll slaughter them –' he swerved suddenly and the circle of children backed off delightedly, cackling with laughter. 'Shove off. Be off,' he cried. 'What is it? A show? Have you paid money to watch, you little pimps? Off. Scram.' He picked up a stone and gestured with it, threateningly, as to a pack of dogs. The children moved. Some went away. Some backed off and followed from a safer distance.

Now they had reached the wall surrounding the mosque. There was a gap in this wall, and here the few people trying to get in were blocked and pushed back by the people streaming out. Farag walked ahead, clearing a path. He kept up a constant dialogue with the crowd. 'Excuse me, excuse me, mother, could you move a little, sister? Just a tiny bit. That's it. Thank you . . . We want to get through, pretty one . . . if you could just . . . that's it . . . that's it . . . Come on, now, come . . .' and so he encouraged them and pulled them through the bottleneck and close to the wall of the mosque itself. They stopped, and the nurse, panting and mopping her face, patted the young man on the chest. 'May God increase your kindness. We'd never have done it without. What a crush. I'd forgotten. It's been so long since I came here, I forgot what it was like.'

He smiled at Aisha. 'Are you all right?'

She nodded.

'It's crowded,' he said, still smiling.

'Yes,' she said.

'You'd better go in. You'll be all right now. It's not crowded inside. I'll wait for you here.'

'May God increase your kindness,' her nurse prayed again.

Now it was she who led and Aisha followed. At the door they stopped and took off their shoes. Aisha looked around for the attendant she was used to seeing at the doorways of the city's historic mosques, but there was none. Her nurse had tucked her slippers, soles together, under her arm. So Aisha did the same and they stepped on to the cool, smooth, marble floor. Darkness and incense, women in black squatting on the white tiles, and a hundred candles burning in front of the gilded grille rising from floor to ceiling at the end of a small room. Aisha followed the black figure of her nurse. Close to, she held, like her, on to the ornate curlicues of the grille and peered inside. Hundreds more candles, thousands, the tomb they surrounded covered in ruched pink chiffon – or was it nylon – set with sequins. Her nurse was murmuring extended greetings and Aisha made out that this was Set Habiba, the wife of Abul Suoud, the Saint. No one could approach him except through her, for she had the only key to his heart, and if she asked, he gave. He denied her nothing. You had to take her into your confidence, speak to her as one woman to another, and get her on your side. Then she would intercede for you with the Saint. She would smile at him and soothe his spirit while you made your plea, and in the gladness of his heart he would answer you and give you what you asked. Aisha pressed her forehead to the grille. 'Set Habiba, I . . .' she hesitated. She glanced at her nurse. The old woman's eyes were closed and she was whispering verses from the Koran. What would she say? 'Set Habiba . . .' The frilled tomb reminded her terribly of bridal headboards and quilts and she glanced up at the wall, half looking for the sprawled and naked female who adorned the bedheads of many Cairo bedrooms. Set Habiba. Some middle-class wife lying stiffly rigid in her nest of pink nylon under the jeering eye of the whore on the wall? But if she 'held the key to her husband's heart', if she 'smiled at him from behind her latticed window and gladdened his soul and softened his heart', then she must have known the secrets of his bed; she must have been warm and soft to his touch; she must have wrapped herself around him when he came to her in the dark and – Fake. Maybe she faked. Have *you* ever faked an orgasm? The liberating finger, severely pointing. She stroked him and smiled at him. She prostrated herself before his manhood, his maleness, his masculinity; she fed his pride and she faked her orgasms and she became the power behind the throne, the keeper of the only key to his heart – stop. Stop. This will never do. Pray. Talk to her. That's what you came here for. Now talk to her. '"I turn to God for protection against the Evil One; in the name of God, the Compassionate and the Merciful."' Yes. Easier to start with a formula. The first verse from the Koran. It can't possibly be wrong. And it's an introduction. And then there will be inspiration. '"Guide us to the straight and righteous path. The path of those who receive Thy mercy. Not those who have aroused Thy wrath. Or those who are forever lost. Amen." Set Habiba. I've come to ask you a favour. I . . . I'm no longer in love with my husband . . .' That was not what she meant to say. Her fingers gripped the grille. 'I want to have children. But I don't know what to do. Maybe . . . maybe it's wrong . . . Maybe I shouldn't . . . but he's a good man . . . he's very fond of me. Everybody says so . . . But I, I . . . I don't want . . . I never want him to . . . but I *should* have a child. Set Habiba . . . there's no one I can talk to. Even my nurse . . . they all say, "You *should* have a child. A child will make you sane." Even my doctor says that. I don't know what to do.' The grille was cold and smooth against her face. And she was weeping.

They circled the tomb of Abul Suoud, the Saint, seven times. They read him verses from the Koran, begged God to have mercy upon his soul and meditated beside his austere iron grille. Aisha could not bring herself to confide in him as she had in his wife. It did not seem proper. She would trust the Lady Habiba to relay her message. She smiled at herself as she stood at the popular shrine, surrounded by peasant women. *They* knew the formulae; they suffered no self-consciousness, no paralysing doubts or facile cynicisms. Zeina fidgeted, preparing to leave, and Aisha panicked: to have come so far and to leave without mentioning the matter to the Saint at all? Supposing his wife forgot? Oh *really* – no, but well, well, just in case. 'Sidi Abul Suoud,' she whispered hurriedly into the grille, 'I promise you a sheep if you solve my problem –' then, embarrassed at the suggestion of bribery in her offering, she explained, 'for the poor. We'll slaughter it in your name, and feed it to the poor.' She stood for a minute, holding on to the grille. 'And I will light a hundred candles, for Set Habiba.' That should please him. Zeina moved slowly sideways towards the door. One last frantic whisper, 'Just please, please, for the sake of our Prophet, help me.' Aisha let go of the grille and sped after her nurse. She caught hold of her arm. Well. There was no harm in it, anyway. What was it, after all, but another version of the games she always played: getting to the phone before the third ring; getting into the flat before the staircase light went out; not treading on the cracks in the pavement. And she had left it vague. Let *them* decide what the solution to her problem was. They were wiser than she. Certainly older. Let *them* decide.

The butcher waited at the doorway.

She had not noticed before the scar across his left cheek; it curved from his temple to the corner of his mouth: a delicate, dark brown line, flanked by the tiny dots of stitches. He smiled. 'You read the Fateha?' The question was for her but it was the nurse who answered, 'Yes, of course. For the Saint, and for Set Habiba.'

He walked between the two women, shepherding them out of the courtyard of the mosque and down the slope of the hill.

'You know, if you like this sort of thing, I could take you to far better Presences,' he said to Aisha.

'What do you mean, better?' she asked.

'Cleaner. More classy. In flats, you know, real luxury stuff. And the women who go are all ladies. Ladies in furs, you know. Diamonds. More your sort of stuff.'

'Why?'

'What?'

'Why would they be more "my sort of stuff"?'

He looked surprised. 'Well. The women here. They're all peasants.'

'What's wrong with peasants?'

'Oh.' He considered.

'I really liked it here today. I liked the music and . . . everything.'

'You didn't dance.'

'How do you know?'

'Well?'

Aisha shrugged.

'Were you frightened?'

'Of *course* not. What would I be frightened of?'

Now he shrugged.

'Can't you walk a bit quicker?' The nurse had not been able to hear the conversation that the two were conducting in low voices and she had grown querulous.

'How are you getting home?' he asked, and when Aisha did not reply he knew the answer: 'You've got a car.' She nodded.

'You drive?' She nodded again. He dropped his voice. 'You know, if you like Presences, and watching people and all that, there's the festival of Sidi Ali next Saturday. You should come.'

'Sidi Ali?'

'Ali Zein el-Abdeen, son of Al-Hussein.'

'So he's the grand-nephew of the Prophet?'

'I suppose so.'

'I've never heard of him.'

'He's the patron saint of my quarter. The Slaughter-house quarter. You've heard of the Slaughterhouse?'

'It's a tough area.'

'I'll look after you. No one can come near you there. It's *my* quarter.'

'And it's his festival?'

'Well, there's a small festival every Saturday, really. But next Saturday is his anniversary: his Nativity. So there's a big celebration. You'll like it. You'll have a good time. What do you say?'

'How do I get there?'

They had arrived at the car.

'I'll get in with you now and show you.'

Aisha unlocked the passenger door and leaned in to open the back door. 'Dada, you won't mind sitting in the back for a few minutes, will you? Farag is going to show us the Slaughterhouse.'

'What do we want to see the Slaughterhouse for?' exclaimed her nurse. 'What's so special about the Slaughterhouse?'

Aisha nudged her into the back seat. 'Well, I've never seen it.'

'There's a lot of things you haven't seen,' cried the old woman as the door slammed upon her. 'Do you have to see everything? How many days are there in a lifetime, then?' The butcher got into the passenger seat and was stretching out his leather-clad legs as Aisha slid in behind the wheel.

'Roomy car,' he said, patting the hide seat. She nodded.

'How should I go?'

'She's always been obstinate.' Her nurse addressed an imagined confidante. 'Once she's got an idea in her head, no one can stop her . . .'

Aisha did not bother to answer, following Farag's directions till they emerged from the narrow muddy street into a large, dusty open space. 'There,' he said. 'The wall on the right is the wall of the Slaughterhouse itself. And that building next to it is the police station. And there,' pointing to the opposite side, 'you can see where there's a passage between those two houses? You go through there and you'll come to a clearing with a coffee house. That's where it will be. Only don't come too near in the car. Park it over there, right by the police station so it'll be safe. You'll be all right. If you don't see me, ask for me. I'll wait for you.' He turned to open his door, but a herd of camels was passing by. He waited.

'Are they going to be slaughtered?' Aisha asked.

'No, they're going to a party,' her nurse exploded from the back seat. 'And *I'm* going to be slaughtered if we're any later than this. Your husband must have gone home long ago. Whatever shall we say to him?'

Farag had turned and was looking at her. Aisha looked back. She had done nothing wrong. There had been no occasion to mention her husband before.

Her nurse clambered out of the car as the last camel swung by. She opened the passenger door. 'Go in peace,' she said. 'We're very thankful for your help at the mosque. We have to go home now. And the lady won't be coming back here.'

He had not taken his eyes off Aisha. 'I'll be waiting for you.' He swung his legs out of the car, stood up and followed the last red-stained camel into the Slaughterhouse.

Saturday

Just like the old days.

Aisha drove along the dark corniche. The river ran beside her, dark and wide, marked by rippling, reflected lights. She had asked Mimi to come with her, but Mimi was going through a period of not being allowed out except with her husband. Two other girl friends excused themselves and Aisha decided she would go alone. She would not take her nurse. For days she had felt the old woman's disapproval. She was as bad as her mother, really, when it came to it. And tonight she would have just fidgeted and frowned and seen danger and cut-throats and insisted on going home early. Zeina did not like Farag. Once he had seen them through the crowd, it was obvious that she no longer saw him as a protector but as some sort of parasite; an opportunist grabbing a ride in a posh car. She had thought he was making passes at her. That was why she had made that final reference to her husband. 'Mind,' she had said when they were alone in the car, 'he's not like men you know. He's not like those foreigners or the boys at school or the Gezira Club. You don't know anything about his type. I *come* from a family of butchers and I know how their minds work. He must have thought it strange that you were there in the first place. *Then* you let him ride in your car and talk of going to the Nativity with him. Of course he'll get ideas.'

Aisha laughed. 'I don't know how you can think that. What did I do to give him ideas? He was just pleasant and polite and it was his territory so I accepted his protection. So it gave him a thrill to shepherd us around and to ride in the car. So what harm will that do? He can't possibly think anything. I mean, he saw the car and everything . . .'

'You think that just because you're the daughter of a "family" and he's a butcher he won't even dare to think about you? You're wrong. His mind won't work that way. He sees himself as a master butcher. It's the best trade to be in, these days. He probably makes thousands. "Judge a man by his pocket," he'll think. And he's young and he's not ugly. And you seem to have taken to the dust and the peasants and the Slaughterhouse. "Why not?" he'll think. "Why not?"'

'You've always been scared of everything,' Aisha declared, 'examining disasters from every angle before they've even happened. Well, you made sure he knew I was married, didn't you? So what are you afraid of now? He can't be thinking anything now, can he?'

Her nurse curled her lip. 'You don't know *anything*, do you? I swear by God that you don't know a single thing.' Then she had kept silent.

So now it was just like old times: when she used to escape from her parents, an alibi carefully arranged, to go to a dance or a party. Innocent enough jaunts they were, like this one, and really, there would have been no need for secrecy at all had people been reasonable. The only difference was that this time her nurse was not happy. But then, when had she been happy? She would not tell, and that was what mattered. And if she told? Better and better. Let things come to a head. Let them all know she would do as she pleased and there was no harm in it. Let them know there were more ways of being in this world than the way they chose. And let them know she was not content with the way mapped out for her. Not that she wanted to go to Presences and dance every day of her life. Just that she wanted them to know that there were people, thousands, maybe millions, who spoke to their demons with more familiarity than she did to her husband. Who hoarded and spent hard-earned money on appeasing those demons and keeping them happy. 'And so what?' they'd say. 'Everyone knows about that. Read any text of social anthropology. They are ignorant, primitive people. What's new?' 'And what about the girl who came out of her coma?' she would challenge them. Her parents would smile and her husband look sceptical. 'I'm not making it up. It happened. No one told me about it. I saw it.' Her mother would produce some literary anecdote: Cathy tapping at Heathcliff's window, perhaps. Her father would make a statement on hypnosis and suggestibility. And her husband would laugh: 'We've just had a metaphysical patch, a few days ago. Isn't it too soon for another one?' And if he were in a good mood he might pat her head. Oh, he was so sweet – sometimes. And clever. And funny. She had so wanted to share her adventure with him. She had mentioned her visit to Sidi Abul Suoud and had waited for him to question her, but the questions never came. And so it was not too difficult to decide to go to the Nativity of Sidi Ali without telling him.

Aisha

She was so close to me during that drive. The closest she had ever come. I was glad no one was with her, for I felt we needed to be alone. I could see that she was learning, that she was moving towards me. And meanwhile I was content to wait. I watched her. Her husband was right when he complained she had a sense of drama. She loved to dress the part. I lingered over her black silk dress, falling those few decent inches below her knees; on the soft cardigan she wore for protection against the late March night; on the smooth stockings and black high-heeled shoes. And that night her wedding band was back on her finger.

Aisha parked carefully in the shadow of the police station, climbed out, and locked the car. She tested all the doors just to make sure and gave the car a secret, comforting pat. 'I shan't be too long,' she whispered. A few paces away, she looked back. The sleek and polished machine seemed forlorn and out of place among the carts, the squatting camels, the piles of hay and junk. 'I shan't be long,' she whispered again.

She started to cross the dark, littered clearing. Her heels dug into the hardening mud. But it hadn't rained for ages. Sewers. And their smell was mixed up with the smell of slaughter and of the tannery. So maybe the people who lived here didn't mind. Probably did not even notice. She hoped she was dressed right, would not attract too much attention. She grimaced. It was enough just to be here: a woman on her own, and in Western dress. But it would really have been too foolish to borrow one of her nurse's long black *galabiyas*. And she would have had to change in the garage. No. Surely this was all right. No one could object to a plain black dress.

She trod carefully, avoiding the wetter patches, the shit trails of camels, buffalo, sheep and goats, horses, mules and donkeys and the odd dog; the figures huddled under dark cloaks. As she neared the other side, she heard the sound of bagpipes and the thud of drums. She got to the narrow space between the two houses and was instantly caught up in a dense, seething crowd. She knew it would be no use resisting or trying to cut through so she gave herself up to it. She knew it would finally carry her to the heart of the festival; to that centre which was drawing all these people, from distant parts of the country, towards itself. The crowd slowly wound itself down the alleyway, and as Aisha went farther and farther, the smell of slaughter and sewage receded and she smelled the musk and amber of holy incense.

She had now arrived at the end of the alley and was at the edge of the open space which she guessed held the main celebrations. She could see nothing but the high ceiling of the vast blue and red marquee that covered the clearing and the huge and ornate crystal chandelier hanging from its centre. The sound of the drums was deafening, and with them came the voices of hundreds of men in the chants of remembrance. From beyond the drums came the wail of bagpipes. What do I do next? she wondered. She tried an 'excuse me' and a gentle hand on the arm of the man in front of her. But he did not move. She was wedged between two women in black *melayas* who obviously belonged together and were conducting a shouted conversation across and through her. She glanced over her shoulder: as far as she could see the alley was a solid mass of people. She could not get back. She could not even turn around.

Suddenly, her arm was firmly grasped. Farag the butcher was smiling at her side. 'You're late,' he said. 'I thought you weren't coming.' She smiled back at him. Everything was going to be all right. This was his territory and he knew what to do. He would take care of her. 'I've kept a seat for you,' he said. 'Come.' Keeping his hold on her arm, he made a path for the two of them through the crowd. How does he do it? she marvelled. He seemed to make no effort at all. He just moved and the crowd let him through. He drew her with him and the crowd closed again behind her.

They emerged on to an open and carpeted space. Rows of barefoot men performing the religious dance swayed rhythmically on the carpet. At one end the musicians sat on a raised wooden platform: a dozen men holding drums, flutes and bagpipes. Around the dancers one row of people sat on a ring of straight-backed chairs. Behind them, and all around, was the crowd. It stood fifteen or twenty deep, and stretched back into several alleys. Sometimes it surged forward and a chair would get pushed. Its owner would lose his balance, hold on and push back at the crowd with his elbows. The crowd would settle. To one side of this circle was a wooden garden bench over which a patterned woollen camel-saddle had been thrown. Miraculously, it was empty. It was to this that Farag now led Aisha. 'Here's your place,' he said, and there was pride in his voice. 'It was difficult keeping it so long.' For a moment Aisha thought of fleas, then she rebuked herself for pettiness. 'This is wonderful,' she exclaimed, sinking down, and just in time she remembered that women here did not cross their legs. She crossed her ankles instead and drew her legs to one side, smoothing her dress decorously down over her knees. She put her handbag on her lap, rested her hands on it and looked around her.

The smoke of cigarettes and incense hung blue in the air. The men with flutes and bagpipes were resting but the ones with drums were going crazy. Correspondingly, the dancers were moving into a faster, wilder rhythm. There were all types of men on the floor: turbaned men in white *galabiyas*, peasants in brown woollen robes and close-fitting caps, young soldiers in their khaki. Men in uniform grey trousers and white shirts, fat men, bald men, thin men, men with beards and men with moustaches only. Each man had his shoes beside his feet and was swinging the upper half of his body round, eyes closed, brow perspiring, crying out his faith in the eternal life of God to each four beats of the drum. The drummers rounded off their tune and there was a sudden silence as the men sank down to the floor to sit cross-legged, gazing at the carpet, as they wiped their faces and waited.

'It's different from the women.' Farag leaned towards her. 'The men don't get "sent".'

'The women have more fun,' said Aisha. 'Don't you dance with the men?'

'I can't dance in my work clothes,' he said, slapping the thigh of the black leather trousers. 'It would show disrespect. I meant to change into a white silk *galabiya* for you but there wasn't time. I was afraid you'd arrive early. So I just hosed down and came straight here.'

'Oh, I'm sorry,' said Aisha. 'Have I ruined your evening?'

'Oh no, of course not.' He beamed at her. 'You've made it. I don't really like this dance anyway. It's too tame.'

The musicians were starting again. A different type of music now. The drums had faded into the background and the centre stage was taken by a man playing the two-stringed *rabab*. He drew his bow across the instrument, coughed into the microphone and began the praise of Sidi Ali. He praised his ancestry: the highest and noblest there could be, for his father was the martyred Hussein, his mother was the beautiful and imperious Fatima, and his grandfather was the Holy Ali, beloved cousin of the Prophet.

'Where is the mosque of Sidi Ali?' Aisha turned to her host.

'There.' He pointed. 'Over on that side. You can see one corner and the high window. You could have seen its minaret from the hill of Sidi Abul Suoud.'

'I didn't notice,' she murmured.

She was examining the crowd. The chairs were occupied solely by men – no, there was one woman sitting, apart from herself. She wore a man's striped *galabiya* and her legs were crossed. On her feet were thick black men's socks and golden mules and her head was turbaned in a gold lamé shawl, the fringe dangling on her forehead. Her eyes were heavily lined with kohl and, heavens, she was smoking. The woman turned and stared back at Aisha and Aisha instantly looked away.

The rest of the men looked like dignitaries; community leaders, respected grandfathers and patriarchs. Clean, well-ironed *galabiyas* in silk and fine wool and linen. Starched white turbans, polished shoes, gold-ringed hands resting on the heads of canes. A silver snuff-box being handed around. Any one of them could easily have been her grandfather.

'What are you thinking?' She turned.

Farag was rolling a joint. He read her glance. 'Do you want to smoke?'

'Well . . .'

'You shouldn't really. Women aren't supposed to smoke here.'

'What about her?' She moved her head in the direction of the strange woman.

'Oh, she's different. She's a strongwoman. She can do as she pleases.'

'What do you mean, "strongwoman?" Why? How is she a strongwoman?'

'She just is. She runs her own business. She does as she pleases and she'll never surrender to a man. Even if she chooses to marry someone, she'll hold the right to divorce in her own hands. She's tough. I've seen her beating men up. No one dares cross her.'

Aisha reached out her hand.

'You shouldn't,' he warned.

'Nobody'll notice,' she insisted and took the joint. Really, she was being most indiscreet. But no one here knew her. The crowd would hardly rise in anger and tear her limb from limb because she took a few puffs at a cigarette. And where else would she ever get a chance to try it? She drew a breath, inhaled and held it, then blew it out. She would rather die than cough. Her throat and eyes smarted and she felt her knees go loose, her head expand and nausea rise inside her. She held on to her handbag. So much talk of hashish, and she had never had a chance to try it. Even when a group of her husband's college friends had passed a joint around she had been obliged to hand it on without tasting. For *them* it was daring and bohemian, but for her, oh no, she had to be poised and controlled and look down upon the scene. Well, she did *not* look down upon it. She longed to try. And now she had. She took another drag and this time nausea was the dominant sensation. It's too fast, she thought regretfully, handing the joint back. It's too fast and I'm too harassed. Oh, if I could slowly smoke one with friends. Take it in small breaths, space it out, give my stomach time to settle, then I could follow this delicious, expanding head and see where it would go. But not like this.

He was looking at her left hand as it rested on her right on top of the handbag. He was looking at the wedding band.

In her new light-headedness, she deflected him: 'I thought I might look odd here. You know, on my own and everything?'

'You're not on your own. And no one looks odd here. This is a Nativity. People of all sorts come here. Enthusiasts, madmen, rich people, judges, soldiers. Followers of Sidi Ali. There's a famous army general who comes every year. He sets up a tent, fills it with food, dresses in sack-cloth and feeds the poor with his own hand. I'll take you round the back and show you.'

A trumpet blasted the air beside them. They both turned. A large black horse had cut through the crowd and was pawing the earth behind them. On it was a man with a long trumpet and a black banner. The horse's mane was braided and ribboned and small brass ornaments hung from every inch of his harness. He snorted as the man held him back.

'What's this?' she whispered. 'Who is he?'

'It's the procession of the Shafis,' he said. 'These are their banners. He's clearing the way. We'll wait till their procession passes, then we'll go.'

The procession gathered behind its leader and the crowd parted. The black horse paced slowly out into the open, neck arched, nostrils aflare, eyes rolling. If the rein slackened for an instant, he would surely burst into a terrifying gallop. But he stepped slowly and delicately round the carpet, each foot precisely placed. And following him was the long procession of men on black horses, in black robes, with black banners. Only their turbans were white, and their eyes gleamed in their dark faces as they guided their mounts along the narrow strip that separated the carpeted ground from the row of chairs. Aisha sat still as horse after horse passed in front of her. Seated, her head was not level even with their bellies, and occasionally a horse's leg brushed hers. A confusion of odours: animals and sweat mixed with the faint but ever-present sewage and blood and, containing them all, the sweetness of the incense. It was getting hot, so hot. The horses' bodies were giving off heat.

The crowd was giving off heat, the dancing men. The singer was now praising the personal qualities of Sidi Ali and, from what he said, the Saint sounded more like a strongman than a holy man. 'Behold your virility, Oh behold your strength,' he cried. So hot it was getting. The last horse had passed.

'Shall we go?' asked Farag. She nodded and turned to him, standing up. She did not feel very confident. Or steady.

He looked at her. 'Do you want to eat something? I could get some cheese and eggs.'

She looked at him, surprised. 'No, no thank you. Why?'

'You've gone pale.'

'Have I?' She put a hand to her face. 'It must be the heat and the smoke.'

'Take off your sweater.'

'No. No. It'll pass.'

'Well, let's get some air.'

Again he took her arm and led her through the crowd. He murmured to a boy standing near by and the boy moved to occupy their bench. He turned and smiled, urging her on. 'It's not all like this. It's better away from the crowd.' She followed. He led her by the arm and she kept her eyes down, and all she could see were the black leathered legs and the boots stepping confidently in the mud, and it seemed that suddenly they were out of the crowd and the air was cool and fresh and only slightly coloured by the various smells. They must have come out on the side farthest from the Slaughterhouse, she decided.

Here it was completely dark, but she could make out that there were houses on both sides of the lane. He stopped at one. 'This is ours,' he said. And through a small doorway she could see some crooked stone steps lit by a paraffin lamp hanging from the wall. 'And this,' he pointed to the other side of the lane, 'is where my mother is buried.' 'Here?' she wondered. She crossed over. There were iron railings and beyond them she made out a white stone tomb. Then she saw that there was a door in the railings. She tried it. 'It's locked,' he said. 'My father thinks it's better. But most people don't bother. Come. I'll show you.' They went on. And now the road was no road but a collection of potholes and he put his hand on the small of her back so that she would not stumble. And then he stopped and she stopped and he dug into his pocket and she suddenly said, 'Don't you ever feel sorry for the animal you are about to kill?' and he, surprised, his hand still in his pocket, said,

'No. And I don't *kill* it; I slaughter it. That's different. That's what animals are for; God made them so that we could slaughter and eat them. As long as it's done properly. And I'm an expert. I know what I'm doing.'

'Does it ever try to get away?'

He shrugged. 'No. Not really. It sort of knows, I think. Maybe it's the smell. Or maybe it's so terrified. I don't know. Sometimes a cow will dig its heels in and refuse to move. Then you have to drag it along a bit. But mostly they just come with you. Anyway', he smiled, 'what's all that got to do with you? Here,' he held out his hand, 'sweets for the sweet. Take it.'

Aisha took the sweet from his hand. He watched her

as she peeled off the wrapper and put the sweet in her mouth. Black liquorice. Her favourite. Years, oh years since she'd had it. Since school. She smiled at him. 'Shall we go on?' Again, he put one hand on her back and another on her arm. 'Perhaps we ought to go back?' she said. 'Don't you want to see? It's only a little bit farther.' He led her on. And now it was another open space, surrounded by the same small, bare houses, crumbling against each other. But in the middle there were tombs. Big ones and little ones. And they looked as though they were different colours. '*Tombs?*' she asked. 'Oh these? Yes,' he said. 'Are they different colours?' 'Yellow, blue and green. White gets dirty very quickly.' She moved closer. Clothes-lines hung between one tomb and the next, and clothes were hanging out to dry. On top of one tomb a round tin tray was balanced holding three glasses with tea dregs and a small tin teapot. A figure lay sleeping in the shadow of another. So close. In *her* life she had only been to visit her family tombs twice. And they were far, far away, in the City of the Dead. Here, they were all together; the dead with the living. She turned and looked for her guide. In two days she had learned so much.

Should I have known then? The signs were all there, waiting to be read. Now, of course, looking back, I see that she must have felt something. I knew from the moment she suggested turning back that she had begun to feel uneasy. But I put it down to some final scruple, or even to ordinary fear. My poor, my precious darling.

They walked towards the side of the clearing and there, outside a small, dimly lit café a large woman sat on a chair holding a cat on her knee. The ground around her seemed to heave. Aisha looked at it closely. It swarmed with cats. Tens of them, maybe a hundred, moving silently, slowly; passing over each other, under each other, rubbing against the chair, against the woman's legs. And as she watched, she felt the deep, collective purr that rose from them. She turned to him. 'She's very rich,' he whispered. 'And she's crazy. She thinks they're her family. She controls them. All the cats of the neighbourhood. She decides their lives for them. She'll pick out a male and a female and tell them they're to get married. And they do. She supervises them. And if one of them comes anywhere near another cat, she scolds it and beats it. She even has them hunting in shifts. And the cats do what they're told.' Aisha stood in the dark and stared. The woman was murmuring constantly. The cats purred as she picked them up, stroked them, looked in their eyes and put them down. And they billowed about her feet, wave upon wave, always trying to get closer.

'Come,' he said. Now his arm was round her waist. She tried gently to move away, but he gently tightened his grip. They walked on. 'Why didn't you say from the start that you were married?'

'What start?'

'Right from the start.'

'There *was* no start. And there was no occasion.'

He said nothing and they walked on. 'Where's your husband tonight?'

'Oh, he had to . . . entertain some people.'

'What does he do? A doctor? A diplomat?'

Oh please, she thought. Please don't be like that. 'A diplomat.'

'*Really*?'

'Yes.'

'Well . . .'

'Well what?'

'Does he know you're here tonight?'

She hesitated.

'He doesn't know?'

'Why do you ask?'

'I ask.'

'What's it to do with you?'

'I'm asking.'

'I don't want to talk about him.'

'Why?'

'I just don't want to.'

'Why? Because you're a lady and he's a gentleman – diplomat – and I'm –'

'Please, please don't be like that –'

'Like what? You're the one who's getting angry. Refusing to talk.'

'I'd like to go.'

'To go? Now?'

'Yes.'

'But the celebrations have hardly begun. You haven't seen the snake-charmers, or the banquets or anything –'

'I've seen enough. I really want to go.'

'You *can't* go now. Your seat is held for you.'

'I'm tired. I don't feel well. I really want to go.' She was walking determinedly, even though she did not know the right direction. There were more potholes and more tombs. She stumbled and steadied herself against a tomb. He caught her arm. 'This isn't the way.'

'Then show me the way.'

'You can't go now.' He was pressing her close against the tomb. His hands gripping the tops of both her arms.

She pulled her head back and it struck stone. Pain shot through her temples and her eyes. 'I have to,' she cried.

He put a hand on her mouth. 'You'll make me look a fool going back there on my own.'

She bit. He pulled his hand back and hit her face. Her head struck stone again. He held her head steady by her hair and tore the woollen cardigan open. She realised she was still clutching her handbag under her arm. She dropped it and hit him. He held her head against the tomb and pulled her hair so she felt her neck would break. He reached down to pull up her dress. She tried to knee him but now his knee was tightly wedged between her legs and he was pulling at the zip of his leather trousers. 'No,' she whispered, 'no,' but he named the name of God and thrust and her body received him. He thrust and she fought but she never screamed, even though he had taken his hand from her mouth long ago. Conspirators, in silence they fought a deadly battle. Then his face was buried in her neck and whether she opened her eyes or closed them she made out the stars in the black sky and she cried out and his hand came down again upon her mouth.

183

Aisha

December

It is the end of the year and the cold is bitter. The floor of the small, private clinic gleams in the fluorescent light. The light shines down upon red tubes, white masks and silver steel. And on the operating table. On the table, Aisha lies dying. She has fought, as she knew she should, for the sakes of her loved ones, but now she does not mind too much. No one knows yet whether her child will live.

And now I will have to start waiting again. Perhaps for years. Perhaps longer. But I know she will come back to me. Aisha. She always does.